# ONE GOLD TRIQUETRA

## DOMINANT CORD, BOOK 3

### SADIE HALLER

QTP

ISBN-13: 978-0993826450

ISBN-10: 0993826458

## ABOUT THIS BOOK

A decade ago, a bad play-date turned composer Ella Hudson off BDSM.

Now she's been offered a performance opportunity too good to pass up, but it means working closely with Jackson and Griffin--world class musicians, lovers, and Doms intent on adding her to their relationship.

While Ella struggles to deny her true desires, maintaining her vanilla facade becomes increasingly difficult as the men re-introduce her to a world she'd written off.

~ **Books by Sadie Haller** ~

***Dominant Cord***

One Gold Heart

One Gold Knot

One Gold Triquetra


***Tainted Pearl***

Tainted Pearl

Tainted Shadow


***Frisky Beavers***

Prime Minister

Dr. Bad Boy

Full Mountie

Mr. Hat Trick (coming 2017)

*For my dear friend A.*
*Thank you for always being there.*

Jack set his toy bag down with far more care than his temper demanded. "Dammit, Griff, I thought this one had promise."

"I know, babe." Griff leaned in and touched his forehead to Jack's. "Look, do you really think we need a beard? Sully knows the score and he's cool with it. Do you honestly think Wil and Finn will care? I'm fucking tired of sneaking around. You like to fuck me, I like to fuck you. So what? It's nobody's business but ours, and I don't like constantly having to produce a third to camouflage our relationship. Don't get me wrong, I'm always happy to have some subbie pussy around to torture and fuck, but not to keep up appearances. It makes me feel like I'm not good enough."

Jack brushed a gentle kiss over Griff's lips. "Idiot. You know it's more than just fucking. I love you. You're way beyond good enough; you're everything to me. However, the reality is, neither of us subs, so even if we outed ourselves, we would still need a submissive if we wanted to play at Finn's parties."

"You're right, but I'm fed up with playing musical subbies. This one seemed like she might work out, you know? I don't understand how I could have been so blind."

"Don't go taking all the credit. I was just as blind. She took everything we dished out and begged for more. Maybe I was more wilfully ignorant than blind. Can you imagine how deeply we could have got involved with her if that business with Hildy hadn't happened tonight? All the trouble she could have caused for us? I feel queasy just thinking about it."

"We sure dodged a bullet with that one. Speaking of Hildy, what's the deal? Wil is notorious for going out of his way to avoid newbies, yet he shows up to a play party with one?"

"Not our business."

"I know, but I don't think we've ever had a newbie at a party before. Even Mac had some previous experience."

"Again, not our business."

"You're no fun."

Jack grabbed the hem of Griff's shirt and lifted. "Oh baby, I'm lots of fun."

ONE

Griff smiled wide as he followed Jack into Finn's music room. "Sully, you old slacker, it's about fucking time you got back to work."

"I figured if I didn't show soon, I'd be looking for a new gig."

"Does this mean you're back in full swing?"

"I don't know about full swing, but I've been swizzling the hitty-sticks a little. Fucking busted ribs completely crimped my style."

Griff just about swallowed his tongue when Mac walked in wearing nothing but clover clamps on her nipples and leather cuffs on her wrists. His head was full of questions, but when Jack caught his eye, he nodded and kept them to himself. Not his business.

Sully, who considered everything his business, was not so polite. "Nice outfit, sweetie. Special occasion?" Mac glared at Sully and slowly flipped him the finger.

Griff held back a chuckle when he spotted Finn leaning against the door jamb. Oh, for a bowl of popcorn.

"Oh dear. What an unfortunate turn of events, my love." Finn walked across the room, sat in his chair, and patted his hands on his thighs. Mac stalked over to him and laid herself across his lap.

He reached down and grabbed the thin wooden cleaning rod for his flute. "Before we begin, why are you being punished?"

"I was disrespectful."

"Yes, you were. I accept that you and Sully have a special understanding, but when I have your submission, you must be respectful to everyone, regardless of your normal dynamic. It's not like you don't know any better. We've had this same conversation before. What was your punishment last time?"

"Ten strokes with your hand."

"And what happens with repeat offences?"

"Double the last with whatever implement you choose."

"That means it'll be twenty with the cleaning rod. Colour, Mac?"

"I'm green."

"Good enough. I'll keep count. Do not move." Finn placed his left hand on the small of Mac's back before taking the first stroke. He laid stripe after stripe across her ass, never striking the same spot twice. Mac's facial contortions and tears were the only sign of her struggle to accept her punishment. By the time Finn was done, her ass was striped like a candy cane. "All done, love. Now go apologise to Sully, and once your slate is clean, we will continue with what you were supposed to be doing before this little interlude."

Mac rose from Finn's lap and accepted the tissue he held out. She took a moment to wipe her tears and blow her nose. Then she went over to Sully, knelt at his feet, and rested her forehead on his knees. "I'm sorry."

"All is forgiven, sweetie. I'm sorry too. I shouldn't have teased you." Sully leaned forward and kissed her head. Mac looked up and smiled, then rose to her feet and returned to Finn.

"Good girl. Hands behind your back and turn around." As soon as her back was turned, Finn clipped her cuffs together and kissed her shoulder. "Off you go, sweetheart."

Griff caught Sully's eye and raised an eyebrow as Mac sat on the piano bench. Sully shrugged and shook his head slightly. How the hell were they supposed to have a productive rehearsal with a naked, decorated Mac in the room? More to the point, how was Finn going to concentrate on the music when most of his focus would be on his sub who would be teetering on the edge of her limits?

"Holy shit, if I'd known it was bring your sub to work day, I would have brought Hildy. She and Mac would look so cute sitting on the piano bench with their tits clamped togeth—"

The colour drained from Mac's face, and Finn flew to her side as he snapped at Wilson. "Enough." He unclipped Mac's cuffs and gathered her into his arms. "Sweetie, I fucked up. I'm so sorry." As he left the room with Mac, Finn turned to the rest of the group and said, "You guys go ahead without me."

Wilson stepped towards them. "Mac, Finn, I'm—"

"Not right now, Wil. I need to take care of her. Maybe before you leave..."

Wilson ran his hand through his hair. "Yeah, sure."

As soon as Finn and Mac were gone, Sully pounced. "Dammit, Wil. What were you thinking?"

"I wasn't. It just slipped out. What was going on, anyway?"

"My best guess is Finn was pushing at Mac's issue with the piano bench and figured doing it during rehearsal with a room full of Doms was the best way to do it. He probably would have been right if he'd thought to give us a heads up. He's usually more on the ball about this kind of thing."

Taking pity on Wil, Griff spoke up. "Don't beat yourself up about it, Sully was rather indelicate himself and Mac's reaction earned her a candy-striped ass."

Sully had the decency to look a little sheepish. "Yeah, I think Griff and Jack are the only ones who haven't caused Mac pain of one kind or another today. Right, I guess we should get on with it. What are we playing first?"

TWO

As soon as the front door snicked shut, Jack was up against the wall, and Griff was kissing him like his life depended on it.

Jack grabbed Griff's shoulders and pushed him away. "Whoa, what's this all about, babe?"

Griff leaned back in and thrust his hips forward, grinding them into Jack's groin. "I'm horny."

"That's obvious, but why?"

"What do you mean, why? Since when do I have to have a reason to be horny?"

"We've been together for almost as long as we've been members of Dominant Cord, and not once have you ever tried to jump me the minute we got home from a rehearsal. So, I ask again, why?"

"I guess it was watching Mac submit to Finn—at least before it all went to shit in a handbag—it was beautiful and sizzling hot. It was love. I want that for us. It made me horny."

"You don't think we have love that makes you horny?"

"Are you being purposely obtuse? Our love makes me all kinds of horny. Sharing a sub with you makes me all kinds of horny, too. But I think having a mutually loving relationship with a sub would make us complete. And before you get all pouty, you know as well as I do that we'd probably end up killing each other if we didn't have a sub to torture, and you love pussy just as much as I do."

Jack had no idea what to make the whole situation. He trusted Griff absolutely, but he had a tiny, nagging doubt he could not shake. Sudden changes in behaviour didn't happen without a reason, and Griff got that horny from witnessing a monogamous, heterosexual, Dominant/submissive interaction—not the homosexual interaction waiting for him at home.

It wasn't that long ago he'd wanted to out their relationship to the world, and lately, he'd stopped banging on about it. Did he really want a bi-sexual, poly relationship or was he looking to go straight? He knew Griff's comment about killing each other if they didn't have a sub was meant to ease his concern, but it only did the opposite.

Despite his fear for his relationship, he decided to smooth things over. "Okay, I get it, but I think we might be asking a bit too much of the universe. How many people are lucky enough to find one perfect love, let alone two who also have to love each other? It's a tall, tall order."

"Doesn't make it impossible, though."

Jack stroked a finger along Griff's cheek and brushed a gentle kiss on his lips. "No, you're right. It doesn't make it impossible." He leaned in for another kiss as he took hold of Griff's hand and guided it to his erection. "But see what you do to me? That's all because of you."

"Aw, fuck! Just because I haven't jumped on you after rehearsal before doesn't mean you don't get me all hot and bothered. Rehearsals take it out of me, and after blowing my horn for hours, I'm not in much of a mood to blow anything else, not even your perfectly delectable trouser trumpet."

If only Griff would shut the fuck up. Every time he opened his mouth, he made it worse, and Jack had to wonder if Griff's subconscious had taken control of his mouth. He wasn't usually this insensitive. They say to fake 'til you make it, so Jack decided to brazen it out and not let his hurt show. Instead, he dropped to his knees. "How about I blow *your* perfectly delectable trouser trumpet instead."

By the time he'd made the offer, Griff had his jeans at half-mast and his cock on parade. "Now you're talking."

Jack held Griff's cock at the base as he swirled his tongue around the head, occasionally darting to the centre to lap up the pre-cum. He continued to tease until he felt hands at the back of his head—Griff's way of telling him it was time to get serious.

He opened his mouth and sucked on the knob, alternating between strong and gentle. Jack fought the increasing pressure at the back of his head that was forcing him farther down Griff's cock.

"Fucking goddammit, Jack. I'm in no mood for being teased."

Jack pinched the inside of Griff's thigh and pulled away from his cock. "And I'm not a fucking sub you can order around. Blow your own fucking horn. I'm going to bed.

---

STANDING with his jeans around his knees and his rapidly deflating cock swinging in the wind, Griff wondered what the fuck just happened. One minute, he's well on his way to blowing his load down his lover's throat, the next, he's left hanging without a clue. Past experience, while rare, had taught him to leave Jack alone and wait until he was asleep before joining him in bed.

Griff pulled up his jeans and refastened them. He took a quick trip to the kitchen to grab a beer, then he retreated to the living room and flopped on the sofa.

No matter how he looked at it, he couldn't figure out what had set Jack off. Yeah, watching Finn push Mac to the edge of her limits and how beautifully she submitted totally got his motor running, but did it really matter what got him all charged up as long as he spent the energy at home? Surely there had to be times when Jack came at him with all cylinders firing because he had been turned on by something external to their relationship. It couldn't be the idea of adding a female sub to their mix. Jack had been pushing for that for years.

Griff switched on the television and zoned out. He was done trying to figure out what the issue was. Jack was both a grown up and a Dom, and as such, he had a responsibility to communicate.

An explosion on the TV startled Griff awake. He

checked his watch and figured Jack would be asleep. He hated it when Jack fucked off to bed in a huff. It didn't happen often, but when it did, life tended to really suck for a while. At least he'd be able to get some sleep before he'd have to deal with Jack's next wave of anger.

He crept into the bedroom with his arms outstretched to help him feel his way to the bed. He'd already stripped and taken care of all his needs in guest bathroom to reduce the risk of waking Jack.

He was momentarily blinded by the sudden glare of the bedside lamp. "Quit your fucking creeping around, Griff, and get into bed. I'm tired."

Shit. "I didn't want to wake you."

"Bullshit. You waited until you thought I was asleep so you could avoid any more conflict. It's what you always do. This time I didn't bother pretending to be asleep so you could avoid me."

"What the fuck is that supposed to mean?"

"Did you honestly think I would be able to go to sleep before I knew you were safely in bed with me?"

"I thought you were over that."

"Well, I'm not. Getting called in the middle of the night to come to the hospital because you were injured in a car accident *after* I'd gone to sleep knowing you were safe here at home is not easily gotten over, dammit."

"Look, I've apologised for it time and again. I don't know how many times I've promised to never leave the house when we've had a fight, but you still keep throwing it in my face. It needs to stop. I get it. I made a promise. At some point, you're going to have to trust me to keep it."

"And at some point, maybe I will. But I'm not there yet. Now come to fucking bed, I'm tired."

Griff climbed in and Jack shifted away from him.

"Oh for fuck's sake, seriously? You would rather risk falling out of bed than touching me? Grow the fuck up."

Jack moved farther away and Griff was done fucking around. He slid in behind Jack and slipped his arms around him, dragging him tight to his own body, then shifted them both towards the middle of the bed. "Please stop. We're both tired and running off at the mouth. We can fight in the morning if that's what you want, but please stop for tonight."

Jack's muscles relaxed and he let out a long sigh. "Fine. Goodnight."

"I love you, Jack. Only you. You're my heart." The cold silence he got in return launched a steady stream of tears that continued long into the night.

JACK LAY AWAKE, waiting for Griff to stop his fucking crying and fall asleep so he could get away from him. He knew Griff was upset that he hadn't reciprocated his declaration of undying love, but the truth was, he was really struggling to trust Griff. While he *had* kept his promise not to leave the house after a fight, he thought about the stuff Griff had said earlier, and it had him feeling less and less confident about the security of their relationship.

After what seemed like hours, Jack couldn't stay put

any longer. As he tried to gently extricate himself, Griff hugged him tighter. It finally got to the point where he didn't care whether he woke Griff up and hurt his feelings. "For fuck's sake, let me go. You're smothering me."

Griff sprung away. "God forbid I should fucking smother you. I'm going to sleep in the guest room. I'm not leaving the house, so sleep or don't sleep. I really couldn't give a flying fuck." He shot out of bed and slammed the door on his way out.

Jack lay there wondering how they could possibly consider bringing a third into their home when their own relationship was on such shaky ground.

He flicked the lamp on and grabbed his book. Sleep would be impossible without Griff in bed with him, and it was either read or stare into space all night. He'd barely started his second page when he heard the door creak. He looked up to see Griff's sheepish grin. He returned it and flipped the duvet back. "Come to bed?"

Griff bounded across the room and slipped in next to Jack. "I'm sorry."

"Me too. Let's go to sleep. We can talk in the morning, okay?"

"Yeah, okay."

Jack was just drifting off to sleep when Griff insinuated himself between Jack's legs. Normally, he would be thrilled to have a warm, wet tongue traversing the length and breadth of his cock, but this was not hot make-up sex. This felt more like suck-up sex—an attempt to wash away the anger and upset from earlier. It made him want to puke. He reached down and pushed Griff's head away. "Stop. Just stop. I'm exhausted, and we agreed to go to sleep."

Griff pulled away and settled in next to Jack. Close, but not touching. As he finally drifted off to sleep, Jack wondered how they were going to fix this, and more importantly, did he want to?

GRIFF REACHED for Jack as he did every morning upon waking, and for the first time in all their years together, Jack wasn't there. They'd had fights before. Long, drawn out, vicious fights, but even if they went to sleep without resolving the issue and a rousing bout of make-up sex, Jack was always there when he woke up. Something was seriously wrong.

He climbed out of bed and slipped on his robe. He didn't normally worry about wandering around naked, but if he and Jack were going to hash this out, he wanted some kind of armour. He sniffed for signs of coffee. There were none. Not good at all. His nagging bladder was over-ruled by his sudden, urgent need to find Jack.

He raced through the house, his panic increasing with each empty room he encountered. He finally found Jack in the guest bathroom, sitting in the tub. His knees were pulled tight to his chest and his face was buried in his arms.

The sight shredded Griff's heart. "Hey."

Jack raised his head, revealing his blotchy, tear-stained face. "Is there nowhere in this fucking house I can be alone?"

"Give me thirty minutes to get some shit together and

you'll have *everywhere* in this fucking house to be alone." Griff turned on his heel and stomped out.

He headed straight to the en-suite to finally empty his bladder and gather his toiletries as he frantically tried to figure out where he could go. Those who had space didn't know about his relationship with Jack, and Sully— the only person who did know—barely had enough space for himself, let alone a house-guest.

Who was he kidding? He wasn't the type to impose. He'd be better off in a hotel. He'd get his ass out of the house first, then worry about accommodations. He considered leaving Jack a note, but decided to text him once he was settled. He'd let Jack worry for a bit before easing his mind.

He took a final look over his shoulder as he headed out the door. He'd hoped Jack would stop him before he could leave. With a heavy sigh, he pulled the door closed, the soft snick of the latch, his only goodbye.

THREE

THE FUCKER PROBABLY WANTED SOMETHING. That was usually why he called. The phone continued to ring in her hand and Ella was seriously tempted to let it go to voice-mail. If she didn't answer, she couldn't say yes to whatever favour he'd ask. In the end, curiosity won out. "Well, hey there, Sully, it's been an awfully long time. What's up?"

"Ella, my darling, I have the perfect venue for that piece of yours."

"And which piece would that be? I'm not exactly a one hit wonder, you know."

"While that is true, I only know of one piece you've written that couldn't be scored in a Disney film."

"Oh, that one. Really? You've got a venue for it?"

"Yeah. Friends of mine are having a kinky commit-ment ceremony of sorts on August 16, and I immediately thought of your piece. So, are you interested?"

For once, Ella didn't have to lie. "Of course I'm inter-ested." It was the one piece she'd written and never heard played. "Give me a second while I check my calendar." She reached across her desk and flipped the pages of her appointment book. "You're in luck, it's one of the few dates I do have free this summer. Hold up—venue is one thing, but it won't play itself."

"How many parts are there, and do they all need to be played by percussionists?"

"I suppose we could get by with one percussionist if we had three reasonably coordinated musicians with a decent sense of rhythm."

"I've got a quintet full of Doms to draw from, so I guess we just need the percussionist."

"If you don't have someone in mind, I know one who'd be perfect. I just need to confirm availability."

"It's your piece, so you would know best. That said, I think it would be a good idea for you and the percussionist to meet with Mac and Finn ahead of time. It's their celebration, and it's crucial that they are completely comfortable with all the attendees—for obvious reasons."

"No problem, but I tend to have weekdays more open than evenings and weekends. Do you think we can work something out to fit with that?"

"Absolutely. Just get back to me with a few times and dates that will work for both you and your percussionist, and I'll set it up."

"Will do. Thanks for this, Sully. You've just made my day."

"Always happy to help, my sweet. Now we have business out of the way, let's get caught up. You're right, it has been far too long and I have been a bad and neglectful friend."

They'd talked for more than an hour by the time Ella punched the end button on her phone. She'd tried to ignore the stab of guilt when he told her about his busted ribs. It *had* been forever since they'd been in touch, and even with her crazy schedule, she should've made some time for her friend.

She thought back to the reason for his call and let herself get a bit excited. She'd been sitting on that piece for years, and quite frankly, she had expected to be sitting on it until she died.

She needed to call Teagan to double check her availability, but first, she wanted to reacquaint herself intimately with the piece before she discussed it with anyone. She didn't have any difficulty locating the file. Even if she hadn't kept meticulous records, it was the one piece she'd never lose.

Her journey through the piece brought the memories, both good and bad, flooding back.

## FOUR

Sully answered the door and swept Ella into his arms. "You look gorgeous, my sweet." He laid a loud smacking kiss on the top of her head and gave her another squeeze.

Fortunately, Ella was prepared for the moment Sully noticed Teagan, because he dropped her like a hot brick. She tried not to let the laughter bubble out when she saw him practically drooling at the sight of Teagan's perfectly pedicured bare feet as she slipped them out of her ballet flats. He was so easy. Teagan was already his type, but with that raging foot fetish of his, Ella, knew he'd be a sucker for some bright red toenails. No, she wasn't above a little manipulation.

"Sully, I would like introduce you to Teagan Fitzpatrick. She's the percussionist I told you about."

From the way Sully's gaze kept bouncing between Teagan's offered hand and her bare feet, Ella was a little worried he might skip the niceties and drop to the floor to kiss her feet instead. Thankfully, his professionalism won out. "Pleased to meet you, Teagan," he said as he shook her hand. "If you will follow me to the living room..." Sully shot Ella a wide grin and turned to lead the way.

The room full of people took Ella by surprise. She had only been expecting to meet with Mac and Finn. She shot Sully her best annoyed look. He just shrugged in typical Sully fashion and led them towards the group. She'd almost forgotten that Sully was more of an ask forgiveness than permission kind of guy.

He pointed to each person as he made introductions. "Ella and Teagan, I would like to introduce you to Finn and Mac, the happy couple. Wil, Griff, and Jack will be the other percussionists, and Hildy, Lucy, Karen, and Jenn will provide the playing surfaces. Everyone, this is Ella Hudson, our composer, and Teagan Fitzpatrick, our percussionist."

Mac stood and took Ella's hand in hers. "Welcome. Sully's told us about your piece, and I have to say, I'm thrilled that the world première is happening at my little shindig."

"I'm glad it's finally getting to see the light of day. Did that miserable reprobate tell you it's been rotting in my bottom drawer for a good ten years?"

"He did. He was like a kid at Christmas who couldn't wait to play with a new toy. I shit you not, his eyes sparkled and he rubbed his hands with glee at the prospect."

Ella laughed. She had no problem conjuring up that image. She had seen it enough times in person.

Ella continued to chat with Mac, occasionally glancing at Teagan to make sure she was okay. She needn't have worried. Sully was being the perfect host, and things looked promising. She turned her full attention back to Mac, and was startled to see they'd been joined by Jack and Griff. She looked back and forth between the two. "Uh, hi." Oh, she was fucked. Actually, she wasn't, and not likely to be, but her panties were soaked. They were both far too tempting.

By the time they'd each flashed her a saucy grin, her panties were in such a state, sitting was no longer an option, and she still hadn't decided which of them posed the greater risk to her self-control.

Griff offered his hand, and the rich timbre of his voice made her want to drop to her knees. "Hi, I'm Griff. I'm looking forward to playing this piece of yours."

"Ella, hi." Oh, how she hated these kinds of things. The awkward meetings and uncomfortable silences. She got more than enough of those when she attended performances of her work. Ella disengaged her hand and was immediately offered another to shake.

"I'm Jack. Pleased to meet you, Ella." Aw hell, Jack's voice would be every bit as effective at getting Ella to submit to anything as Griff's.

"Likewise." What the fuck was that? Who, in this century, says fucking likewise? She tried to ignore the resulting blush that burned to the tips of her ears. She just smiled and waited until she could politely reclaim her hand.

"Oh, pack it in, you two," Mac warned. "Come on Ella, let's get something to drink."

Ella nodded and followed her host. Once they were in the kitchen, she said, "Thanks. I have no idea what the hell just happened there."

"*That* was two Doms trying to claim the same territory." Mac grinned and opened the fridge. "Help yourself."

Ella grabbed a can of Coke and leaned against the counter. "I'm *so* not Dom territory. I will admit to experimenting back in the day, but it wasn't for me." The lie tasted bitter on her tongue.

"Oh dear. Considering your piece is called *Rhapsody in Black and Blue for Instruments of Ass Destruction* and involves hitty-sticks and naked flesh, I got the distinct impression you wouldn't have a problem attending our celebration"

"Crap. I'm sorry, I should have been more clear. While I'm not interested in participating, I don't judge, and I'm perfectly fine with others participating around me. Besides, this will probably be its only performance, and I won't do anything to jeopardise that."

"Fair enough." Mac patted Ella's hand. "If you're comfortable, I'm comfortable. I'm assuming Teagan knows what to expect from the piece and the performance?"

"Yeah, you have nothing worry about there. There are a bunch of reasons why I recommended her."

"Not the least of which, faith she and Sully would hit it off?"

"Busted. I was hoping I'd been subtle."

"I've been trying to get Sully settled for years. One look and it was obvious to me he's his match. "

Ella grinned at Mac. "So far, so good."

"You do realise, I'm going to do everything I can to help this along."

"I'll take all the help I can get."

"Help with what?"

Fuck. Like her panties weren't soaked enough already.

Mac turned. "Nothing that concerns you, Griff. Don't you have somewhere else to be?"

"Nope." Griff flashed another cheeky grin at Ella.

"Look, Ella and I were having a private conversation, so if you do not mind…"

"I can take a hint. Just let me grab a beer, and I'll be out of your hair."

Mac rolled her eyes and smiled at Ella as they waited for Griff to leave.

He grabbed a beer from the fridge and shrugged. "I'll see you both later, then."

As soon as he was out of sight, Mac giggled. "You like him."

Ella groaned. "No."

"Oh, come on, tell me you didn't just cream in your panties."

"I can't tell you that, but I've already told you, he's not for me." The pang of disappointment was hard for Ella to ignore.

"If you don't sub, then you're right, he's definitely not for you. He plays hard."

"Who plays hard?"

"Oh for fuck's sake, Jack. If we wanted to include you and Griff in our conversation, we wouldn't have escaped to the kitchen."

Ella needed to get the fuck out really soon. She was having enough trouble coping with her ridiculous attraction to Griff and Jack, but conflict, no matter how trivial, was something she couldn't cope with. "It's okay, Mac. I need to get going anyway." She drank the last of her Coke and placed the can on the counter with the other empties. "Is there anything else we need to go over?"

"But you just got here," Mac protested.

"I know, but I'm on a deadline." Ella knew it was a flimsy excuse at best, but it wasn't really a lie, more of an exaggeration, and she needed to get out of there before the panic set in.

"I understand. I'll walk you out" Mac placed a hand on Ella's shoulder and gave Jack the stink-eye as they walked past.

Ella scanned the room for Teagan as she entered, and was not surprised to see Sully had her backed into a quiet corner on the far side of the room. She and Mac exchanged knowing smiles.

As Ella and Mac approached, Teagan raised her eyebrows. Sully turned around and said, "There you are. Teagan and I have been getting better acquainted."

"Look, I need to head out, I have a lot of work to do." Ella paused a moment. "Teagan, I'm sure someone can give you a lift home if you would like to stay longer."

"I'd be more than happy to drive you home," Sully blurted out.

Ella had to stomp hard on her mirth and didn't dare look at Mac as an image of Sully bouncing up and down with his hand in the air, screaming, "Ooh, ooh, pick me, pick me!" popped into her head.

"I appreciate the offer, Sully, but I think I will head back with Ella." Ella knew Sully didn't have much experience with rejection, and Teagan turning down his offer pretty much guaranteed he'd keep trying.

FIVE

Jack lay awake in his bed. Alone. Again. Still.

What a completely shit week it had been. He had gone from blissfully attached to miserably single in the space of a few painful hours. He hadn't believed Griff would really leave until he heard the roar of the engine. His heart shattered with Griff's broken promise.

When the realisation hit, he'd immediately climbed out of the tub and pulled the plug. He'd tried not to panic as his mind catapulted him back to the last time Griff left home angry.

He'd been asleep in bed when the call came and launched him into a nightmare. He'd had to shake the cobwebs from his brain and process the horrifying news before he could function, wasting precious minutes he could have spent with Griff in the hospital.

The hours he'd spent waiting for the phone to ring since Griff's departure, were unbearable. The longer it was silent, the more frantic he became. The fear and anger had his gut churning so much, he'd spent most of that time dry-heaving in the toilet.

A measly two word text: *Not dead*, finally arrived more than four hours after Griff had left. If the situation hadn't been so fucked up, he'd have probably laughed. Instead he sobbed with relief.

They hadn't talked since. Sure, they'd spoken when necessary to keep up appearances, but they hadn't actually *talked*.

Rehearsals were the worst. It was like some twisted comedy. Guys who were together but pretending they weren't, are now no longer together and pretending nothing's wrong while they're not together.

The house was no longer his safe refuge. Was it ever? With Griff gone, it no longer felt warm and inviting. He missed Griff's laughter. The silence was suffocating.

The one small bright spot in his week disappeared as quickly as she'd arrived. If they'd met Ella before that epic fight, they'd be lying here together, plotting the best way to make her theirs. Considering how fast Griff had moved in on Ella this afternoon, he was probably busy plotting the best way to make her his alone.

The horn solo from Bach's B Minor Mass blared through the silence. Think of the devil, he's sure to appear. He flicked the light on and grabbed his phone to read the text. *Call me?* His heart banged and his fingers fumbled as he stabbed at the buttons.

Griff answered on the first ring, but didn't speak. Jack waited. By his reckoning, it was Griff's turn to do something, and the mere act of answering the phone didn't rate.

He glanced at the screen. One minute and forty-three seconds. If Griff didn't say something by the time it hit two minutes, he was hanging up.

"You still there?"

Jack took a deep breath as he willed himself to be civil and not voice all the snark bouncing around inside his skull. "I'm here. What's up?"

There was a heartbeat of silence before Griff cleared his throat. A sure sign he had been crying. "I miss you."

Jack didn't know how to react to Griff's admission. Wants and needs bombarded him at warp-speed, but acting on any of them would make him more vulnerable. He was barely holding it together as it was. He didn't know if his heart could survive another stomping. As tears streamed down his face, he scrambled for the right thing to say—for both of them.

Another deep breath. "I miss you, too." The truth.

More silence.

They had been together long enough for Jack to know when Griff was working his way up to something difficult. Griff had made the first move, so he could be patient.

"Can I please come home?"

Fuck. What they wanted and what they needed were not even close to the same thing right then, and Jack hated being the bad guy. He took a moment to gather his thoughts.

"I understand how hard it was for you to ask, and I want to say yes. I really want to, but we've got to work through how we got into this mess so we can find a way out of it. If you come home before we do that, I'm concerned we'll fall into bed, fuck like bunnies, and be so disgustingly happy in the moment, we'll shove this mess into a closet and forget all about it until one of us trips the latch and it all spews out and buries us.

"To be perfectly clear," Jack continued, "I would love nothing more than to do exactly that, but I think we need to sort through our issues first. My heart can't bear a repeat performance of the last week."

"Not even if I sleep in the guest room?"

"It has nothing do with where you sleep. You know as well as I do, we'd end up fucking the minute you walked through the door."

"Then how are we supposed to work this out?"

"We meet in a public place."

"Can we do it soon?"

"Ten o'clock tomorrow morning for coffee at Brewster's soon enough?"

"Can we make it eight?"

Jack looked at the clock. It was already three. "You want to do this on five hours sleep?"

"I'll be lucky if I manage two. I can do ten if that's what you need."

"No, I'll be there at eight. Goodnight."

"G'night."

Jack wondered about Griff's motivation as he slipped his phone back on the bedside table and switched off the light.

Would Griff have contacted him tonight and asked to come home if they hadn't met Ella? It bothered him that he would probably never know the answer. It bothered him more that it mattered.

GRIFF SAT at the table in the far back corner of Brewster's. He hadn't been able to sleep and had arrived shortly after they opened at six. He checked his watch for what must have been the thousandth time since he first sat down. It was still half an hour before they were supposed to meet, but knowing Jack, he could turn up any minute. He went to the counter and ordered two coffees so he could have one waiting for Jack as soon as he arrived.

He had no idea how they were going to find a way to fix the problem, when he didn't have a clue what the problem was.

This past week had been unbearable and he was exhausted. Sleep had been elusive, and when it did finally come—it was short-lived and disturbed.

He'd let his temper get the better of him, and he was paying for it. Instead of spending the week sleeping in Jack's arms, he'd spent it in an empty bed with nothing but his right hand for company.

The pettiness of making Jack wait hours before letting him know he was okay was among the shittier things he had done in his life, but he felt most awful for breaking his promise and leaving angry. He'd completely blown Jack's trust in him and he'd do anything to earn it back.

The door opened, and Griff thought his heart might fall from his ass. Jack looked as bad as he felt. Worse, maybe. He half stood and raised his hand to get Jack's attention. Their eyes met, and Jack returned Griff's shy smile as he made his way to the table.

Nerves took control of Griff's mouth "It's fresh and

hot. I just sat down with it a minute ago. It's exactly how you like—"

Jack placed his hand on Griff's shoulder as he sat. "Hush, you're babbling. Thank you for the coffee. Is all that shaking because you've been here drinking coffee since opening, nerves, or both?"

"What do you think?"

Jack smiled. "Definitely both."

They sat in awkward silence for the longest time before Griff finally mustered up the courage to speak. "I've gotta level with you, Jack. I have thought of nothing else, but I'm feeling pretty clueless about what the hell happened."

Leaning forward, Jack held Griff's gaze. "I've to ask you something, and I want you to think about it for a bit before you answer. Okay?"

Griff didn't like the sound of this at all. "Okay?"

Jack closed his eyes for a minute, then took a long sip of coffee. Griff's gaze drifted to Jack's throat muscles as he swallowed and he wished his cock could be right there. Jack lowered the mug to the table and Griff returned to reality.

"This is important, Griff, so please give it serious thought before you answer. I'll understand if it's something you'll need more time to think about than we'll spend here."

"Just spit it out, you're making me even more nervous."

"Are you looking to go straight?"

That was the last question Griff expected. "What. The. Actual. Fuck? Where would you get that idea?"

"After that rehearsal—"

Well, shit—he was back to that again? "I got horny

after witnessing a beautiful act of submission between a straight couple, and somehow my love life magically becomes no boys allowed? I don't need any time to think about this at all. While I thought I'd made all this clear that night, I guess I didn't, so let me spell it out for you.

"I love you. It is *that* simple. We both have appetites that can't be sated within our relationship. I thought we'd agreed to indulge them as needed, and if the opportunity presented itself, open up our relationship in a way that would permanently fulfil these needs. In other words, my understanding of our relationship was you and me first, and we'd add a third only if the right female sub came along. Replacing you with a woman is never, ever going to happen.

"If you want to remove the option of a third, then let's do that. If I can only have one person in my life until the day I die, I want that person to be you."

"But you got horny after—"

"And I came home to fuck you. Except, as I recall, that didn't happen. There will be times where something outside our relationship will get me horny. If you're honest, the same goes for you. Regardless of what popped my pecker, you're the only place I park it."

Jack chuckled and Griff breathed a little easier. He still had an apology to give, and with the ice broken a little, now was probably the best time. "Jack, I'm really sorry about leaving angry and making you wait to know I was safe. I broke the only promise you've ever asked of me, and I know earning back your trust will not be quick or easy, but I need to know it's possible and that someday you will forgive me."

Jack pushed his mug towards the centre of the table and rose from his chair. "Go get your stuff, I'll be waiting for you at home."

---

As MUCH AS Jack wanted to drop to his knees when Griff walked through the door, Griff would need to assuage his guilt, and bottoming to Jack tended to work best for both of them.

He spent the ride home in the car choreographing their first encounter. While there would be lots of make-up sex where they would take turns being bottom and top, that wouldn't happen before Griff was free of his guilt. God only knew what it would take for that to happen. Griff had never broken a promise before.

He considered and dismissed scenario after scenario. He was almost home by the time he had settled on a plan of action. He didn't anticipate having much time to prepare before Griff arrived. Chances were good that he had already checked out of the hotel, taking a gamble on Jack inviting him back home.

Jack parked the car and hurried indoors. He'd barely finished getting organised before the doorbell rang. What the fuck was that about? He'd expected Griff to walk in and had planned accordingly. Oh well, he could be flexible.

He closed his eyes for a moment and composed himself, then opened the door. "Inside. Leave your stuff by the door, strip, then kneel in front of my chair. Safeword is red."

Griff cocked his head to the side like he always did when he thought Jack had said something outrageous.

"I'm not playing around, boy. If you want my trust and forgiveness, you'll have to earn it. If a sub broke a promise and risked her life like you did, you know she would be severely punished until she'd learned her lesson. What makes you think you deserve less?"

Griff lowered his eyes and shifted from foot to foot, but remained silent.

"I gave you instructions, I won't tell you again." Jack walked to his chair and sat. He hoped his relief didn't show when Griff finally entered the house and closed the door. He'd spent those awful seconds of waiting, frantically trying to figure out what to do if this plan went to shit in a handbag.

Jack's cock grew harder with each garment Griff removed. The cheeky fuck was doing a slow strip-tease. Fair enough, he'd only told Griff to strip, not how to do it. A week without coming was sure taking its toll on Jack now. If he'd known what was in store, he might have taken the edge off. Then again, he would much rather get off down Griff's throat than in his own hand.

Finally Griff was down to nothing but a sultry smile. He sauntered across the room and sank to his knees in front of Jack.

"Good boy." Griff growled, and Jack grabbed him by the chin. "Silence. I don't want to hear a sound from you unless it's your safeword or to answer a direct question. I don't anticipate giving you any reason to do either. You can nod for yes and shake for no. Understand?"

Griff nodded. Jack let go of his chin and stood before undoing his jeans and releasing his angry cock.

"Good boy. Leave your hands by your sides and open your mouth. You'll take it all. Tap my leg three times if you need to safeword." Jack placed one hand behind Griff's head and fed him his cock in one long, slow glide. Once he'd reached the back of Griff's throat, he held his breath and waited a moment to allow Griff to prepare before continuing deep into his throat. Once Jack had his balls resting on Griff's chin, he put his other hand behind Griff's head held it tight to his groin. He had absolute control and Griff was going to have to trust him. That would be the first step to rebuilding their trust in each other.

Jack held Griff's head in place until he was starting to feel a bit uncomfortable, but nowhere close to his limit. Griff had an enviable lung capacity and it was always him or Sully who won breath holding contests. Jack let go and pulled his cock from Griff's mouth before he released his own breath. Breath play was tricky. He rarely indulged, but when he did, he never took uncalculated risks.

Jack stroked the top of Griff's head. "For being such a good boy, you may use only your mouth on me any way you like provided you make me come within the next two minutes and swallow every drop I give you."

Griff took the head of Jack's cock in his mouth, and sucked hard as he swirled and flicked his tongue. Occasionally he took Jack's entire length and swallowed a few times before backing off. Finally, he bobbed up and down in short fast bursts until Jack couldn't hold back any longer. Along with his semen, he pumped a week's worth of anger and hurt down Griff's throat. When Jack was spent, Griff released his cock and laid a gentle kiss on the tip. He looked up and flashed Jack that irresistible grin of his.

"You cut that pretty close, boy." Jack chuckled. "It's a good thing you succeeded, because you wouldn't have liked the consequences of failure. I'm going to need a little time to recover for the next round. So how about you go put your things away and you can join me for a nap when you're done." Griff nodded and Jack left for the bedroom.

Jack opened one eye and spotted Griff standing in the doorway. "Stop walking on eggshells, boy. You rang the bell, and now you wait to be asked into the bedroom? Firstly, as long as you have a key to this house, you have no reason to ring the bell. Secondly, I had already told you to join me when you were done. The invitation had been extended, there was no need to wait for another." Griff crossed the room, and Jack opened his arms wide. "Come and snuggle."

As soon as Griff was close enough, Jack wrapped his arms around him and pulled him close. He hoped he'd pushed Griff hard enough to erase his guilt so they could move on to the make-up sex. "I forgive you, babe. Trust is going to take some time, and until I'm there, I want you to give me the keys to your car—no driving. Can you do that?" Griff nodded. "Are you out of guilt yet?" Griff nodded more vigorously. "In that case, let's get things back to normal."

"Honestly, I'm forgiven?"

"Honestly."

"Thank you." Griff cocked his head and raised his eyebrow. "You know, I'm happy to give up driving, but you do realise you'll have to be my chauffeur until you give me back my keys."

"If it means I know you are not dead or mangled in a ditch somewhere, I'm good with that."

"I do love you, Jack. I need you to know you really are my heart. I let my temper get in the way, and I hurt you, and I'd do anything to take it back. I don't ever want to do anything that will make you feel like you aren't the most important person in my life."

"I'm getting there. I want it to be true, and when the trust is there, I'll know it to be true. Until then, I can't promise not to hold back a little."

"I don't like it, but it's my own fault and I understand."

Jack leaned in and touched his lips to Griff's. "I love you. You are my heart." He leaned back in and with the next kiss, he bared his soul.

---

GRIFF WOKE and grinned as he realised he was in his own bed and all snuggled close to Jack. He still couldn't believe Jack had gone all Dom on his ass and made him submit. Thinking back on it, though, Jack was right, he carried guilt long and hard, and this fuck-up was by far the worst of his life, and he'd had some doozies. Last time he had self-imposed a guilt-trip, all he had done was accidentally bleach Jack's favourite black t-shirt, and it was three days of grovelling before he felt like he had made amends. Of course, it was all his own baggage. In the grand scheme of things, Jack couldn't have cared less about the shirt, and as hard as he tried, he failed to convince Griff he was blowing the whole thing out of proportion. He turned to look at Jack and was surprised to see his eyes open.

Jack leaned over and kissed him. "Good morning, babe. You were thinking awfully hard. What's up?"

"Oh, I was thinking about how you handled me when I came home yesterday."

"And?"

"It surprised me, but after some thought, it made sense that it worked so well. And before you go there, this is only to be used for extreme situations, and to be clear, I plan to avoid those situations like your life depended on it."

"Good, because I hated every minute of it."

"Not every minute, coming is always enjoyable."

"It was a relief, but for me, enjoying an orgasm involves more than the physical release. "Now, those orgasms that came after," Jack smiled and traced Griff's lips with his finger, "those were most enjoyable." Jack shimmied down the bed and gave Griff's erection a long, slow lick from root to tip.

As much as Griff wanted to come, this morning he needed a connection he couldn't get from a blow job. "Babe, I don't care who's on top, but I want to see your face, to kiss you, to gaze into your eyes and show you just how deep my love is for you."

Jack popped up to the head of the bed and rummaged in the top drawer of the bedside table before straddling Griff's thighs. He opened the condom and deftly slid it over Griff's straining cock. "Here," he said as he handed Griff the bottle of lube, "you drive."

Griff laughed and bucked his hips, knocking Jack off balance enough to gain the advantage and reverse their positions. He slathered plenty of lube over his cock, then he positioned the tip at Jack's anus and applied steady pressure until he was fully seated. He lowered himself until they were nipple to nipple, then he gave Jack a long, languorous kiss. "In that case, it is time to blow out your carbon. You've been driven far too gently, lately."

Jack's eyes lit up. "Floor it."

Griff withdrew and held the head of his cock against Jack's entrance. "Vroom, vroom." He gave a couple shallow thrusts, then snapped his hips forward and pistoned in and out of Jack's body at an unforgiving pace. He stared into his lover's eyes while he covered his face with gentle kisses.

"Griff, I can't hold back."

Griff brought his mouth to Jack's for a soul-searing kiss as he increased the speed and force of his thrusts. Jack's long moans of ecstasy as he fell over the edge were all Griff needed to send him hurtling off his own cliff. He collapsed over Jack's body, breathless, his heart pounding. "I need a minute."

Jack chuckled. "No hurry, I could stay like this all day."

"Be careful what you wish for because my cock is already on board with that idea. I need to turf the condom and we need to clean up. What do you say to a shower?"

"Yes please."

SIX

Ella laughed when she saw the name on her phone. Of course it was Sully. She was just surprised he had waited two whole days before calling. "You're looking for the skinny on Teagan, aren't you?"

"Perhaps."

"You may have her number, but only because she told me you could."

"Seriously, that's all I'm going to get?"

"Since when have I ever been one to divulge information about others?"

"Since never, but there's a first time for everything."

"Not when it comes to other people's business."

"And to think I have interesting stuff to share with you about Griff and Jack."

"I'm sure you do."

"Hey, sweetie, what's wrong?"

"Nothing, it is fine. I've gotta run. I'll text you Teagan's number as soon as I hang up, okay?"

"Yeah...thanks. I will talk to you soon."

"See ya."

Ella focused on the wind-chimes tinkling outside her window. She let their happy music soothe away the rising panic. The only time she was ever able to stand up to anyone was in defence of others, but doing so always took a big toll.

Trust Sully to pick up on her interest in Griff and Jack. Yes, she was curious, but she couldn't afford to risk her safety because they made her heart go pitter-patter. Besides, how could she possibly choose between them? They were both tall and beautiful, with killer grins and voices so deep and gravelly, she'd obey without a second thought. Of course, looks weren't everything. Her limited experience told her the prettier the face, the bigger the asshole, and life was too short to spend it choosing between the lesser of two assholes. If only her pussy were as sensible as her brain.

She thought back to that awful, terrifying night and the last pretty boy she'd played with and strengthened her resolve. No romantic entanglements of any sort. She had enough scars—emotional and physical.

SEVEN

Jack set the two mugs of coffee on the kitchen table and settled onto the chair next to Griff. Even though their reconciliation was new, he felt better about their relationship than he had in a very long time. It would probably be better for both of them if he brought up the subject, and morning coffee was as good a time as any. "So, uh…Ella?"

Griff had just taken a swig from his mug and fought not to choke. "What about Ella?"

"What do you think?"

"I think you're going to need to be more clear about what you are asking."

Jack took a long sip of his own coffee. "Would you be interested in playing with her?"

Griff looked incredulous. "Seriously?"

"Yes, seriously. I told you I was still open to a third, and if the wood you sprung when we met her was any indication, you're just as interested in her as I am."

Griff reached over and cupped Jack's cheek. "Are you

positive? I need you to be more than sure about this because, like you, I couldn't deal with a repeat of the last week."

Jack smiled and leaned into Griff's hand. "I'm sure."

"Then, yes, I would very much like to play with her."

"Excellent. The question is, how do we go about it?"

"Normally, I'd say Sully was our best bet, but he seems kind of preoccupied with Teagan. Considering the way Ella and Mac hit it off, maybe we should see if Mac is willing to help. We can keep Sully as a back-up plan."

Jack nodded and took another mouthful of coffee as he glanced at the clock. "Mac should be up by now." He reached for his phone and punched in the number.

A breathless Mac finally answered just as Jack was organising his thoughts to leave a message.

"Hey Jack, what's up?"

"Um, sorry, is this a bad time?"

"No, not at all. My phone was half-way across the house is all."

"You can call me back when it is more convenient--"

"Spill it, Jackson Riley."

"Are you sure you're a sub?"

"Quit stalling and spit it out."

Damn, she was bossy when Finn didn't have her at his feet. "Griff and I were wondering whether you know if Ella is spoken for."

"She's not your type."

"What's that supposed to mean?"

"According to her, she experimented a little back in the day, and found it wasn't for her."

"Bullshit. You know as well as I do, that piece of hers is a love song, not some ditty about a failed experiment."

"I know no such thing. Look, you and Griff go through subs faster than Wilson goes through clarinet reeds, so even if she *is* subbie material, I don't think she's *your* kind of subbie material. I think she deserves something more substantial than a few hours as the filling in your sub-sandwich."

"Geez, Mac, you make us sound pretty callous."

"Aren't you? I rarely see you with the same sub more than once or twice. It's like the pair of you are trying to blow your way through the city's entire supply."

"I get how it looks, Mac, but if you understood the situation, you might see it differently"

"Then explain it to me."

Jack shot a pleading look to Griff. "I wish I could, but it is complicated."

Griff nodded and whispered, "Tell her."

"Mac, can you hang on just a sec?"

"Yeah, sure."

Jack hit the mute button and set the phone on the table as he looked at Griff. "You'd better be sure, because there's no unringing this bell."

"I'm sure. It's time, and we could probably use some outside help because we're not doing so well on our own. Besides, I think I trust Mac's judgement over Sully's. Especially now he's tripping all over himself sucking up to that percussionist friend of Ella's."

Mac's voice rose up from the table. "Um, fellas, you just rang that bell loud and long on speaker."

Griff picked up Jack's phone and laughed as he looked at the screen. "You tit."

Jack smacked his head and let out a nervous chuckle before he spoke. "Okay, so you heard all that, then."

"Yeah, but it was still kind of vague. If you want my help, you're going to have to make me sympathetic to your cause, so give it your best shot."

---

Mac ended the call and joined Finn in the kitchen. "You are never going to believe what that was all about."

"Try me."

"Well, for starters, Griff and Jack finally outed themselves to me. I suppose I could have made it easier on them by admitting I already knew and it's the worst kept secret in the history of secrets, but they've worked so hard to keep their relationship on the down-low, I didn't want to spoil the surprise."

"It's about time." Finn lifted an eyebrow. "Please tell me you didn't leave them under the misconception that I would still be oblivious."

Mac chuckled. "No. In the end, I took pity on them and confessed that everyone knows and it's no big deal. But that's not even the best part. they're actively looking for a third. A female sub to be exact. They haven't been man-slutting, they've been auditioning potential life-partners."

"No. Way."

"I know, right? But it gets even more outrageous. They both zeroed in on Ella and they want me to help smooth the way for them."

"Bad idea, love. Meddling in people's lives can destroy

friendships. Besides, meddling in matters of love is entirely Sully's purview."

"Normally I'd agree with you, but they said themselves that they trust my judgement over Sully's, especially now that he's been showing so much interest in Teagan."

"Things could have gone very badly when you interfered between Hildy and Wilson."

"I don't think it's fair to call it interfering. I was asked for help. And as far as the situation between Hildy and Wilson, I think it's a prime example of why Griff and Jack called me."

Finn tapped his chin with his finger. "Okay, I'll concede the point, but I'm still not comfortable with this."

"It may well be all for naught, you know. Even though Griff and Jack had her totally creaming her panties—and yes, I asked—their Domliness was a show-stopper. Apparently, whatever experience she had when she was younger was not worthy of repeating."

"Just so I'm clear on this, you're going to help a pair of bi-sexual Doms double-team a woman who has no interest in BDSM?" Finn looked skyward. "Sweet, sweaty Jesus, have you lost your fucking mind, woman?"

"Yes, and maybe."

Finn picked up his mug and took a long swig of coffee. "Baby, please be careful, that's all I ask."

"I'm only going to provide a low-key venue for the three of them to get to know each other better. Everything else is entirely up to them."

Mac huffed and stalked off when Finn started laughing.

## EIGHT

Ella picked up her mug of tea and took a long sip as she tried to process the crazy day she'd had. One minute she was putting the finishing touches on her latest composition, the next she found herself at Mac and Finn's front door, and by the time she'd returned home, she'd spilled her deepest, darkest secret. Enough of it, anyway. One tiny two-letter word and she'd have spent the evening sitting in the comfort of her own home instead of attending a small dinner party at the home of kinky people she barely knew.

When Mac had answered the door, Ella held out the bottle of wine she'd brought and held back a huge sigh of relief. Finn made her nervous. "I hope you like red."

"Oh, I most certainly do like red. How about we get it opened right away so it will be ready for drinking in time for supper."

Ella toed off her shoes and followed Mac to the kitchen, thankful it was empty. "Where are the others?"

"They're all in Finn's man-cave, but I'm almost ready

to serve, so they'll show up any second. I don't know what it is about men and their uncanny ability to show up for food as soon as it's ready, but not one moment before all the work is done. Ha! The joke's on them. They're on clean-up duty, and as you can see, I'm not the clean as you go kind of cook—I'm more of a use every pot, pan, and utensil you can find kind of cook. Truth is, I'm just learning. Before Finn and I got together, my cooking skills were limited to opening a packet and heating it in the microwave."

With the sound of distant footsteps, Mac caught Ella's eye and they both erupted into fits of laughter.

"What's so funny?" Finn asked. "We could hear you cackling at the other end of the house."

Ella and Mac exchanged looks and laughed even harder as Griff and Jack followed Finn into the kitchen. Mac, laughing too hard to speak, pointed to the empty plates and waved her hand at the pots on the stove.

Finn kissed the top of her head. "I think my gorgeous, sexy woman, who cooks the most delicious food, is trying to tell us we should go ahead and serve ourselves."

Mac nodded. She and Ella were just getting themselves under control when Ella caught Mac's eye and the tears and laughter gushed anew.

Finn chuckled. "We'll be in the dining room when you two are capable of making it to the table."

Dinner was an uneventful affair filled with meaningless small talk which didn't do anything to suppress the growing puddle in Ella's panties. Knowing the men were Doms should have squelched her arousal, but it only seemed to make matters worse. Every time she managed to get her lust under control, one of the two would speak to her. Griff had the sexiest way of saying her name and Jack made her heart flutter when he called her sweetness.

At the end of the meal, Ella suppressed a giggle and didn't dare make eye-contact when Mac informed the men, in no uncertain terms, who was in charge of cleaning up and serving tea.

"Grab your wine, Ella, we'll finish it in the comfort of the living room."

Ella picked up her glass and followed Mac. She settled herself on the big leather sofa while Mac sat on the matching arm chair.

"So, what do you think of them?"

Ella knew this was coming. Non-committal indifference. That was the key. "They seem very nice."

"You've gotta give me more than that, Ella."

"Really, they seem very nice."

"Come on, I know they've got you hot. You have been doing the wet-panty-shimmy all evening."

It was time to shut this down. Mac was far too shrewd. "Even if I could decide on one, they are Doms, and as you know, that makes them off-limits."

"What if you didn't have to choose? What if you could have them both?"

Ella struggled against the spit-take before safely swallowing her mouthful of wine and setting her glass on the side-table. "Both? How is that an option? I can't even be with one Dom, two would be impossible."

"Okay, but there's something I'm not getting. How could you write that piece without having any interest in BDSM? Can you explain it to me?"

Ella looked nervously towards the kitchen and took a sip of her wine. "Perhaps another time?"

"Do you mean that, or are you deflecting?"

Ella thought for a moment. "Probably a little of both. I think I could probably explain it to you sometime, but it would have to be in private with no risk of being interrupted."

"I can understand that, but trust me, they're going to be busy with the kitchen for quite some time—I have rather exacting standards and you saw the disaster I left for them. I get the feeling it's a lengthy tale, but we've got time for the abridged version. Besides, it'll make it easier for me to run interference if I know the story."

Mac was right. It was pretty weird to write a piece like that and profess to have no interest in BDSM. She stole another look towards the kitchen before fortifying herself with the last of her wine.

"I did experiment when I was younger, and I loved it until the night I met the wrong Dom. In case you haven't noticed, I don't do well with conflict, and I can't say no. Back then, Sully vetted potential Doms and monitored my scenes. One night, I went to the club on my own because he was busy and I didn't want to wait until he had a night free. I was over-confident and had developed a raging case of sub-frenzy." Ella pulled and twisted the hem of her shirt.

"I met a very pretty man who made me weak just looking at him. We played at the club and it was amazing. I went home with him because I wanted the night to go on forever. Within minutes of arriving at his house, I would have given anything for it to end. It did, but not until almost dawn. He loaded me into his car and dumped me, naked and bleeding just inside my front door. Truth is, I probably would have gone home with him anyway because he asked, and I wouldn't have been able to say no."

Mac joined Ella on the sofa pulled her in for a hug. "I'm so sorry. What did Sully do about it?"

"He didn't know—still doesn't. He doesn't even know I went to the club that night. It was my own fault. I got what I deserved."

"Oh, sweetie, I don't need details to know it wasn't your fault, and you definitely didn't deserve what that bastard did to you."

Ella wouldn't argue the point, so she nodded and pulled herself together.

***

JACK SPENT the whole evening keeping a lid on his anger, but the moment Ella's car left the driveway, he exploded. "Abused? Some self-serving prick claiming to be a Dom abused her?"

Griff laid his hand on Jack's shoulder. "Calm down. What are you talking about?"

"I overheard her telling Mac why she's not into BDSM. She met a guy at a club who showed her a good time until he got her to his place."

"What else did you hear?" Mac asked.

"Nothing. Guilt from eavesdropping got the better of me, and I returned to the kitchen."

Mac frowned. "She believes what happened is her own fault and she deserved it."

Finn wrapped his arms around Mac. "And you set her straight?"

"You bet your favourite cane, I did. Not that it did any good," Mac smiled at Griff and Jack, "but I think I know a couple of Domly fellows who'd be more than willing to do the necessary convincing."

After a nod from Griff, Jack said, "We're in."

"She was sparse with the details, so my understanding is based on what she's said and the way she acts. She's unable to say no to anyone, and it seems she'll say and do anything to avoid conflict, including outright lie."

Griff took Jack's hand and gave it a squeeze as he spoke. "Toxic behaviour in a D/s relationship, but not unmanageable."

Jack smiled at him and squeezed back. "Griff's right, and regardless of whether she turns out to be the third we're looking for or not, we'll do what we can to help build her self-esteem and find more functional ways to handle conflict. I do have a couple of concerns we need to address. The first is Sully. From what you've said, he's completely oblivious to the situation. When he finds out, he's going suffer guilt of Catholic proportions and we'll need to find a way to mitigate it. He'll be the next best thing to useless if he's busy beating himself up over something he had no control over."

"Secondly, she's terrified of us. Completely understandable, but we're going to have to come up with a way to help her feel more comfortable."

Finn spoke up. "One thing that should help is her presence at rehearsals. She'll see the care with which you treat the subs you're playing in her piece. That said, you'll need to treat them exactly as you would any other sub. I think it's important for you both to come across as the genuinely caring guys you are, not as a pair of pretty boys looking to impress."

Mac picked up from Finn. "Exactly. From what she described, her abuser was on his best behaviour and pulled out all the stops to impress her. If she gets a whiff of anything like that from either of you, it's game over.

"I think Finn is on the right track with Ella being present at rehearsals, but there won't be all that many between now and the performance, so I think we should also invite her to most of our group activities. As evil as it sounds, we can take advantage of her inability to say no. She'll get used to being around the two of you in a safe, nurturing environment. If we invite Teagan along as well, I think she'll feel less like saying no, because she'll be able to help nudge Sully and Teagan together."

Jack chuckled. "Ms. Wallis, you have a rather wide manipulative streak, of which, until this evening, I was blissfully unaware."

"Mac's manipulative streak is admittedly large, but she usually exercises it judiciously. I think, in this case, it's well warranted." Finn pulled Mac in for a squeeze and laid a loud, smoochy kiss on her lips. "Given all dealings with Ella are likely to fall on Mac for the next little while, maybe you two can handle things with Sully?"

Jack and Griff exchanged nods and stood. "Not a problem. Now we have the beginnings of an action plan, I think it is time Griff and I head off."

Griff flipped down the quilt as Jack's erection preceded him into the bedroom. "Is all that for me?"

Jack smiled and grabbed the base of his cock. "For now, but if things go our way, you're going to have to share."

"Mmm, I'm looking forward to sharing, can you imagine having it buried deep inside Ella's pussy while I lick and suck on your balls?"

"I can. But right now, I would prefer reality over imagination."

Griff climbed out of bed and knelt in front of Jack with his hands at his sides and his mouth open wide in anticipation. He looked up into Jack's eyes and saw the love. As Jack slid in, Griff relaxed his throat and moaned, prepared to take every inch Jack had to offer. He loved the way Jack's fingers tangled in his hair and held him in place as Jack tilted his hips forward and slowly buried his cock deep before easing back to the entrance of his throat.

"Baby, I'm going to come in your mouth, then I'll do anything you want."

It wasn't often Jack gave him Carte blanche, and he only ever asked for one thing. This time Jack was in for big surprise, and Griff could not wait.

Jack increased the pace and force of his thrusts until he finally clutched Griff's head to his groin and emptied his balls down Griff's throat. He untangled his fingers from Griff's hair and gently stroked his cheek as he withdrew. He grabbed Griff's hand and helped him to his feet.

Griff leaned in and brushed a kiss over Jack's lips. "You know what I want, don't you?"

"Of course I do, it is what you always want when I offer to do anything."

"What if I didn't ask for it this time?"

"Why?"

"Because maybe I love that you are willing to do something you hate more than I love you doing what you hate. Does that make sense? Coming so close to losing you put a lot of things in perspective."

"I don't hate it. I just don't love it."

"Don't start lying to me now, Jack."

"Okay, you're right, I do hate it."

"I know. However, just because I'm not asking for a rim job this time, doesn't mean I won't ask the next time you offer me anything I want."

"I know. If you're not going to ask me for a rim job, what would you like?"

"I want to make love with you." Griff put Jack's hand on his own erection. "I can't wait to be inside you. Go lay on your back on the bed, I'll be right behind you."

After Jack settled on the bed, Griff gathered what he needed from the drawer in the bedside table. He rolled on the condom and popped the lid of the lube before squeezing a generous dollop in his palm and slathering it over his cock. He grinned at Jack and settled into position. "Are you ready, love?"

"Please."

Griff leaned in, letting his weight and gravity provide the slow steady pressure. As he felt the head of his cock breach Jack's ass, he stopped and backed out a bit before leaning forward and resuming his tortuous slide into his lover's body. When he was finally all the way in, he hooked Jack's legs over his arms, and settled into a slow, steady rhythm, every so often, leaning his head in for a kiss, but never taking his eyes off Jack's. "I could do you all night like this, babe. Would you like that, or would you like me to go at you like a jackhammer?"

"Ever the romantic."

Griff slid his cock all the way in and held still. "Just say the word, and I'll bring you flowers and chocolates."

"Damn it, Griff, I don't want flowers and chocolates, I want you to fuck me. Please."

Griff drew back and thrust his hips forward, slamming his body into Jack's. "Like that?"

"Oh God, yeah, just like that."

Griff unleashed, pumping hard and deep. Just as he was ready to come, he released Jack's legs and slid his hand between their bodies and grabbed tight to Jack's cock. He buried his face in the crook of Jack's neck and bit down. Jack's tortured moan and warm spurts of come on his belly set off his own brain-searing orgasm.

Exhausted, Griff barely had the presence of mind to pull out. Jack stroked his cheek before he removed the condom from Griff's cock and headed to the bathroom. Guilt washed over him like the warm, damp cloth Jack slid over his body. "I'm sorry, babe. I was topping—I should be taking care of you."

"Not this time, my love. Sleep. We have lots of plans to make tomorrow."

Griff smiled as his eyes fluttered and closed.

## NINE

Jack ran his hand through his hair, as he waited for Sully to answer the door. He and Griff had spent the last two days discussing the best way to bring Sully up to speed regarding Ella's abuse. He was not convinced they'd come up with the best strategy, but they'd run out of time, and needed to work with what they had. He still didn't know how Griff had managed to manoeuvre him into being the one to talk to Sully. His thoughts were interrupted when Sully finally appeared in the doorway, wearing only a pair of boxer shorts.

"Hey, Jack, what's up?

"Hi. Sorry for dropping by unannounced—"

"Not to mention boorishly early. Fuck, man, if you had to wake me up, couldn't you have at least brought coffee and muffins?"

Jack held up a bakery bag and brushed past his friend. "I'll make the coffee."

"This sounds serious."

"Just go get showered and dressed. I'll have coffee ready by the time you're done."

When Sully walked into the kitchen, the coffee and muffins were sitting on the table. Jack drank from his mug and set it down in front of him. "Have a seat, Dave."

"Oh God, this is serious. I swear, only you and my mother use my first name, and then only when I'm in big shit or something bad has happened." Sully sat and took a long sip of the hot coffee.

"It was years ago, but you are right, something bad did happen." Sully looked stunned, and Jack took advantage of the silence and told him everything he knew of Ella's assault.

Sully slumped in his chair, devastated. "Fuck! That's what happened? I didn't see her for about two weeks after that. Every time I invited her to join me at the club, she had other plans. I didn't think much of it. I'd become kind of blind to her deflection tactics and just thought maybe she had met someone. In a warped kind of way, I guess she did. She was relatively new to the scene and prone to sub-frenzy, which was why I was vetting her Doms, and monitoring her scenes so closely. It didn't occur to me she would go to the club on her own. I should have known better."

"Look, it's in the past and you wallowing in guilt is not going to help matters. Here's the thing. Griff and I really like her, but until she develops some trust, we're not going to get anywhere with her. Regardless of what does or doesn't happen between us, Griff and I want to do whatever we can to help her believe she's not at fault and she didn't do anything wrong."

"I was supposed to protect her."

"You did. You couldn't be with her every minute of every day. Nobody could. Like I said, It's all in the past. We need to deal with the here and now."

"What do you need me to do?"

"Talk to her."

"I'm going to need some time to process this first."

"You have got until the next rehearsal."

# TEN

Ella tried not to let her irritation come through as she answered the phone. Mac's interference was becoming a problem. That weird, uncomfortable conversation with Sully was just the start. Now she's been orchestrating social event after social event that she just *had* to attend. "Where have you decided I should be, and when?"

Mac giggled. "Am I that bad? It is easier to get Sully and Teagan together if they know you're going to be there too, you know."

"No, you're not quite that bad, and you're right, I do want to do whatever I can to nurture their budding relationship." What a joke—that relationship was doing better than fine and didn't need any help. She wondered how much longer Mac would continue trying to set her up with Jack and Griff before finally admitting defeat.

"Good, then you'll join us for a barbecue at our house around four this afternoon."

"Mac, with all your social gatherings, I'm sure I've been spending more time at your house than my own."

"I know, isn't it great? After spending so many years in solitude, it's so nice to finally enjoy a social life and have girlfriends."

Ella was surprised. "What do you mean, solitude?"

"You haven't heard the story? Hell, I thought everyone had heard my sad, pathetic tale of woe by now. My final recital at the end of my first year of university won me a scholarship. One of the oboists from my studio thought that scholarship should have been his, so he decided to punish me. He tied me to the piano bench in a practice room and raped me. Sully saved me and was the only person I trusted enough to let near me as I withdrew further and further from the world. It wasn't until he introduced me to Finn that I started to take my life back."

"I'm so sorry, Mac. I had no idea."

"Different circumstances, but I think it's fair to say we both had good reasons to shy away from BDSM for a while."

"Was the guy a Dom?"

"No, but before the rape, I'd been dabbling in BDSM and I quite enjoyed a side of bondage with my sex. He ruined that for me for a long, long time. I still struggle with stuff, but it's getting better. While I don't know the details of what that asshole did to you, and I don't need to, I want you to understand that I do know what it's like to be terrified to trust another person with your physical and emotional safety. And I'm going to tell you something Sully told me not long after I met Finn. *There are men who are good, and kind, and trustworthy. Men who will treat you like you deserve to be treated. There are men out there who you can be alone with and be safe.* As much as I hate to admit it, he's right."

Ella considered Mac's words. For the first time since that awful night, she didn't feel quite so alone. Sure, unlike Mac, she was responsible for her assault, but if she looked past the difference in circumstances, she could accept that there was someone else in the world who had some idea of what her life was like. "But at least for you, it wasn't your fault."

Mac snorted. "You're right, it wasn't my fault, just like what that fucker did to you wasn't yours. That didn't stop me from blaming myself and trying to figure out what I did wrong, though. Turns out, I didn't do anything wrong —and neither did you. Now, back to more pressing matters. Finn is doing burgers, so are you able to bring a salad? No need to go to any fuss, bagged from the store is fine, as long as we have some leafy greenery."

"I can make a salad, no problem. Is there anything else you would like me to bring?"

"Nope, just your lovely self. We'll see you at four."

"I'll see you then."

Ella disconnected the call and flopped into her chair. She considered Mac's disclosure. If she hadn't said anything, Ella wouldn't have had a clue they'd both been so similarly violated. Mac seemed so comfortable with the men in her life, and she certainly had no qualms about laying into them, even Finn, if the mood struck. Ella wondered what it must feel like to give someone shit without wanting to pass out. She dismissed the thought for the ridiculous notion it was and went to raid the fridge for salad fixings.

GRIFF SPOTTED Ella sitting on the deck stairs, balancing her plate on her lap as she took a big bite of her fully-loaded burger. He caught Jack's eye before joining her. "Do you mind if I sit here?"

With her mouth stuffed with burger, she shook her head and shrugged. He reached over and stole a tomato wedge from her plate as he parked himself next to her. "You sure know how to build a burger. "

Jack arrived and sat next to Griff. They'd agreed ahead of time for one of them to push a little, but leave Ella with a graceful out. "Hey Ella, is he bugging you?"

She took another big bite of her burger and shrugged again.

Griff reached over to steal a piece of cucumber, but Jack gave his hand a gentle smack. "Dammit Griff, it's bad enough when you raid my plate, but now you're being downright rude."

"Oh, I'm sure Ella would say something if she didn't want to share her food with me."

"I'd hope she would."

Ella swallowed her mouthful. "Oh, it is okay, really."

Ella's response revealed how much she would endure to avoid conflict. He caught Jack's eye and he knew they were both on the same page. They needed a new game plan.

Griff turned to Jack and winked as he stole a potato chip from his plate. Jack grabbed Griff's wrist and squeezed until he dropped the chip. "Griff, that's enough. You're being a bully."

"Sorry. I was just messing around."

Ella's eyes went wide as she prepared to stand up "I should go see how Teagan is doing."

Jack loosened his grip, but kept hold of Griff's wrist as he looked at Ella. "No, you shouldn't. Teagan is getting along just fine with Sully. In fact, I think maybe they could use a break from you and Mac using the flimsiest of excuses to thrust them together."

"I should go help Mac—"

"Ella, it's okay. Not all conflict is unhealthy, and it probably wouldn't hurt you to see it resolved. I didn't like what Griff was doing and I called him on it. We sorted it out, and that's the end of it. Nothing bad is going to happen."

"No, really, I should—"

Griff unleashed his Dom-voice. "Enough. There's nothing you should be doing beyond enjoying your burger and a nice spring evening. If you're really that uncomfortable, say the word, and we'll leave you be."

Jack gave Griff's wrist a gentle squeeze and released it. "Ella, it's entirely up to you. It's okay to ask us to leave. Really."

Ella stared at her plate in silence.

"Griff slowly reached out and gently touched Ella's arm. She flinched, but he didn't back off. "I know this is really hard for you, so how about the three of us sit quietly and eat? Nod if you are good with that."

Eyes still on her plate, Ella nodded and took a bite of her burger.

## ELEVEN

Ella couldn't believe she'd agreed to attend Mac and Finn's play party. Well, she could. If only she'd had the back-bone to say no. Of course, truth be known, she was more than a little curious. She'd seen how Griff and Jack handled the subs during those few rehearsals, and found herself wondering if they were putting on a show for her benefit or whether they were behaving normally. The consistency with which they treated the subs almost had her believing their careful attention was standard operating procedure.

She looked at the clock, relieved she hadn't disappeared so long into the void of self-reflection she'd have to rush to get ready. She didn't even know what she was going to wear. Mac told her the dress-code was Dom-defined and because she had no Dom, she could wear whatever she felt comfortable in.

She went to her closet and sifted through garments, dismissing each in turn for being too frumpy. Why had she left this until the last minute? If she'd checked her closet even yesterday, she could have gone shopping for something appropriate. That was the point she admitted to herself she wanted to dress to impress.

Her phone announced an incoming text. She was so frustrated with her quest to find the perfect outfit for the evening, she was tempted to ignore it. She looked back in her closet, then sighed and reached for her phone. The message was from Mac.

*Stop fussing over what to wear. Jeans are fine. Come a little early, and we'll raid my wardrobe for just the right top.*

How the fuck could she know this? Ella's eyes darted around the room, almost sure she'd find a hidden camera. She looked back at the phone and responded the only way she could.

*Ok, thanks.*

She'd grill Mac later. Her only worry now was filling the tub full of hot water and bubbles.

---

JACK NUDGED Griff as he spotted Ella and Mac descending the stairs into the playroom. "Check out our girl. She's even more sexy than I thought she'd be."

Griff looked over and grinned. "Want."

"Down boy. This is going to take some finesse."

"I know, but give me a minute to drool first, will ya?"

Jack held Griff's hand, as much to show affection as to keep him in place. "Let's give her a little time to settle in. Mac said she's not here to play, just to get her bearings a little so she'll be able to cope with all the action at their official cohabitation party."

"I wasn't going anywhere, I just need to make a few physical adjustments. Things are getting a little hot and uncomfortable in my trousers."

Jack shifted to partially block Griff from view so he could discretely rearrange his equipment. He took the opportunity to seductively run his tongue over his lip as he winked.

"Not helping, you fucker."

Jack grinned. "I just want to make sure you are all primed and ready to go the minute we get home."

"I was fucking primed about five minutes after I blew my load down your throat this afternoon."

As soon as Griff was done, Jack turned around and scanned the room for Ella. "Are you ready to go say hello?"

Griff nodded, and they sauntered across the floor.

Mac called out to them as they approached. "Hey fellas, where's your sub du jour?"

Before Jack or Griff had a chance to respond, Finn sidled up to the group. "Careful, love, or I might get the idea you like repeating the no rudeness lesson." Mac looked like she had more to say, but clearly had the wisdom to close her mouth before it got her into real trouble. Finn stroked Mac's cheek and nodded his approval before turning to Jack. "Sully is going to be late, so I was wondering if you and Griff would sit with Ella while Mac and I play?"

Jack smiled at Ella as he answered. "We'd be happy to."

Finn turned to Ella, "Sweetie, I know Mac already

discussed this with you, but, I want to make it clear to everyone—anything to do with you, comes through Mac or me. We have no problem saying no, and we both want you to feel safe and comfortable in our home. Griff and Jack are going to sit with you, and if they think you're uncomfortable with what's going on, they're going to escort you upstairs and away from the action. Safeword here is always red to stop. It works for everything, conversations, situations, and playtime. If you get uncomfortable and call red before these two galoots notice a problem, there's a reward in it for you." He turned back to Griff and Jack. "Do not let her down."

"We won't. Now go play while we help Ella find a spot to get settled." Jack looked at Ella and smiled. "Okay, honey, I'm going to give you some choices. First choice, would you prefer juice or pop?"

"Juice, please."

"There ya go. Nice, easy questions. Griff can you please grab Ella some juice?"

"On it," Griff said as he left for the refreshment table.

"Would you prefer to sit where you can see the whole room or a part of the room?"

"Part of the room."

Jack considered this promising. He would continue to keep conversation low-key and avoid yes or no questions. "Perfect. Would you prefer to watch the side of the room where Mac and Finn are playing, or the side where Wilson and Hildy are?"

"Where will Sully be playing?"

Jack chuckled at the wholly unexpected answer. "I

don't know, but we can move for a change of scenery any time you like."

Griff returned with Ella's juice and Cokes for himself and Jack. "So, where are we sitting?"

"Ella? Finn and Mac, or Wil an Hildy?"

Ella ducked her head a little and avoided his gaze, but spoke up. "Finn and Mac, please."

"Perfect." Jack led the way to a sofa in the aftercare area that had a good view of the space where Finn and Mac were playing. He gestured to the centre of the sofa. "After you."

Once Ella was seated, Jack took the glass of juice from Griff's hand and passed it to her before sitting to her left. Griff handed Jack a Coke and then took the seat to Ella's right.

The three sipped their drinks in a relatively comfortable silence, and Jack kept one eye on Ella as they watched Finn visit all manner of torture on Mac. If her subtle squirming was any indication, leather slapping red ass was a very real turn on for the lovely Ms. Ella. Of course, given the piece she had written, he wasn't overly surprised. He stole a look at Griff and their gazes locked for a moment as they exchanged knowing smiles. Oh, how he wanted to ask her a metric shit-tonne of questions on the subject of leather and bright red asses. Well, really all he wanted to know was how she'd feel about the leather seat-strap from his bassoon on her bright red ass.

Ella sipped her juice and fought not to squirm. She failed miserably, as she felt her panties grow wetter with each stroke of the leather belt Finn laid on Mac's bare ass. Having the two sexiest men on the planet book-ending her only made the situation worse. She thought back to Finn ordering Griff and Jack to take her elsewhere if they thought she was getting too uncomfortable, and she started to worry. What if they mistook her rampant horniness as emotional discomfort and dragged her away? She needed to get herself under control. Ever since she'd resurrected that damned piece, she had been jonesing for some good kink and she desperately wanted to accumulate some decent wank-fodder. Something she had no chance of doing if these guys thought they needed to evacuate her.

She kept waffling between feeling sexy and self-conscious. She was enjoying their hungry looks, but was terrified they would see what she was hiding.

It had been difficult finding something in Mac's wardrobe she thought would adequately cover her scars without being frumpy. She finally settled on a cream stretch lace top. It was sheer enough to give a sense of showing skin, but appeared to have enough pattern to mask the tangle of scars that littered her entire torso. Mac had changed in front of her and when she saw no visible scars on Mac's body, Ella was even more deter-mined to keep her ugliness and shame to herself. On the very rare occasions people had seen her scars, they'd either turned away in disgust or smothered her with pity. She couldn't deal with either reaction from Mac. She'd needed to pee anyway, so she used that as an excuse to get changed in the bathroom. If Mac thought she was weird or a prude, she didn't comment, and for that, Ella was grateful.

She'd been so nervous when she and Mac came down the stairs into the playroom, she'd been frantically trying to think of excuses to leave. Then she saw Jack and Griff. There was no mistaking their hungry expressions for anything less than pure lust. For her. It had been a very long time since she'd felt desirable, let alone lust-worthy. She didn't expect that feeling to last long, so she'd been determined to enjoy it for as long as she could.

"Ella?"

Ella startled from her thoughts and turned to Griff. "Yeah?"

"Can I get you more juice?"

Ella looked down at the empty glass in her hand. "I can get it."

"No doubt, but I asked if I can get you more juice. So, can I?"

Oh shit, there was no question that was his Dom-voice. "Yes, please, that would be lovely, thank you."

"Jack, more Coke?"

"If you don't mind."

"Of course I don't mind. Anything for you, Jack. You know that."

Jack winked and shot Griff a sexy lop-sided grin. "In that case, I have a few ideas for later."

And damn, if that exchange didn't make Ella's scalp tingle and her panties flood. She struggled against her growing need for an orgasm and tried to figure out whether or not she needed to stop for batteries on her way home.

As Griff wandered off, Jack leaned in close and whispered, "Would you like to come, sweetheart?"

And how the fuck was she supposed to answer that? Oh yeah, she wanted to come in the worst way. She kept mentally pinching herself with memories of that disastrous night in order to keep her need in check. What if she said yes? She had no doubt they would make her come, but it was how they'd do it that made her feel anxious. What if she said no? Then she'd have to wait until she got home. A trip that got longer the moment she realised she would have to make a battery stop. She was buggered no matter which answer she chose. Fucking Doms.

"It's a yes or no question, Ella. Do you really need to think that hard about the answer?"

Griff returned with their drinks and sat down. This time, close enough for his thigh to touch hers. "What did I miss?"

Ella felt the heat rise to her hairline, but in a determined effort to pretend the question hadn't been asked, she fixed her gaze on Mac's scarlet ass as Finn continued to wallop it with his leather belt.

"Sweetness, pretending I didn't ask doesn't mean it didn't happen. If you really don't want to answer, you can call red. Finn wasn't bullshitting when he told you red works for everything. I asked the question because you've been getting pretty squirmy, and I'd pretty much bet my Dom-card it's because you're horny and itching for an orgasm.

Ella shrugged, hoping that would be enough to make Jack stop.

"Not good enough, Ella. Clear words are the only

thing that work, and in case you have forgotten, your three word choices are, yes, no, and red. Communication is non-negotiable in Finn's playroom, so if you insist upon silence, we'll err on the side of caution and interpret it as a safe-word and take you away from the play area. Oh, and one other thing—honesty is always, always rewarded. So, sweet Ella, would you like to come?"

Ella squeezed her hands into fists and curled her toes. God, how she wanted to come, and she sure as shit, knew she didn't want to go upstairs and miss all the action. Even if he hadn't sweetened the pot for an honest answer, lying wasn't an option—that would mean saying no. "What kind of reward?"

Jack smiled at her. "It usually depends on the situation. In this case, I don't think I can fairly answer that question until I know what your truthful answer is. How about this? You give me a hypothetical answer, and I can give you an example. Would that work?"

As hard as she tried, Ella couldn't really find a problem with it. She could tell the truth and find out what it would get her without having to admit the truth first. "Okay. I think I can work with that."

"Excellent. So, *hypothetically*, would you like to come?"

Ella squirmed a bit more. Damn, that voice was deadly on her won't power. If she wasn't careful, he could get her to do all kinds of things she'd normally baulk at. "*Hypotheti-cally*, yes."

"Then, *hypothetically*, if you were feeling brave enough to let Griff and me give you an orgasm, your honest answer would earn you a second, and just to make it interesting, no toys, and you'd get to keep your clothes on."

It was all Ella could do not to burst out laughing. Two orgasms? She figured she had hit the jackpot if a man could find her clit without a sat-nav and a flood-light, let alone make her come. As for doing it while she was fully clothed and without toys? In what universe? They seemed so cocky, it was almost tempting to let them try just to see their egos crash and burn. Sully would be arriving soon, and he'd make sure she was safe. Besides, by her calculations, the worst that could happen was no joy, and she'd have to wait and take care of her own happy ending when she got home. At best? Double the pleasure with a fraction of the wait. "That's a pretty *hypothetically* tempting reward."

"How about a real answer to the question, love?"

Ella picked at her cuticles and chewed at the inside of her cheek. Was she really going to do this? She cast her thoughts back through the weeks since she'd met these men. She considered their behaviour, then weighed it against what she had been told by Mac. Taking all that into account, they *seemed* genuine and trustworthy enough.

She thought about the last pretty boy she'd trusted. He'd seemed genuine and trustworthy too. That was when she learned her judgement was defective. It was an expensive lesson, paid for with the tangle of silvery lines that marred her skin. A permanent reminder of unbearable pain and terror.

Then she considered the differences between the situations. That awful night, she was on her own. She hadn't had any outside input about the pretty boy. She'd never seen, let alone played with him before that night. He'd exhibited impeccable behaviour the whole time at the club, but she hadn't listened to that little voice in the back of her head reminding her never to go home with a stranger, especially without taking any safety-precautions like arranging a check-in call or texting his address to a friend when she arrived at his house. No, sub-frenzy had done a spectacular job of ignoring that little voice.

On the other hand, she'd seen these guys in action at rehearsals, and their care of the subs they played was always safe and consistent. In addition, Mac vouched for their character. That had its pluses and minuses, though. Yes, Mac had been through a similar experience which impaired her ability to trust, but as far as she knew, Mac had never played with Griff and Jack, and even if she had, it was pretty obvious Finn would be paying close attention, not willing to put Mac at even the slightest risk.

Of course, she was ignoring the obvious. Regardless of what they might be like with a sub in private, she was surrounded by people who would keep her safe. Hell, she'd have to be a complete idiot to give up the potential for two orgasms, neither of which, would be self-induced.

She looked from Jack to Griff and considered their patient, but hopeful expressions. Dammit, she was going to do it, she was going to let her pussy do all the talking. Again. "Yes."

* * *

Griff grinned at Jack and stood. "You two talk, I'll go get things organised."

Jack reached over and gently took Ella's hand. "I appreciate that you told the truth, sweetheart, but I can see you're terrified. I want you to understand, Griff and I would never do anything to harm you, and we'll do everything in our power not to scare you. I know you and Mac talked about past experiences, but I want you to know, all she told us was that you have good reason not to trust. She never told us what it was. She said you'd tell us if and when you felt the time was right. I also understand that it's going to take way more than words for you to believe this to be true. Griff and I are more than keen to do whatever it takes to prove it to you, but we can be patient for as long as you need.

"We want to give you those orgasms, but it's pretty clear to all involved you're not going to stick up for yourself, so we're going bring in a referee once our options have finished playing for the night. You can clarify your limits and any concerns with Mac. More anticipation on your part will do you good. So, the question is, should we ask Finn or Sully to officiate. Jack's attention shifted as Ella began picking at her cuticles again. He studied her fingers, the skin around her nails was ragged where she had chewed them. This was a destructive habit they would need to work on, but it could wait. There were so many more important things to tackle first.

"I'd like it to be Finn. I don't think Sully is up for it."

"Good enough, love. Now, while we've got some time to kill, and the opportunity to chat, I'd like to know more about that delightful piece we're rehearsing. What inspired it? If I'm to do it justice in performance, I think I should know its background."

Ella took a deep breath. "I'd have thought Sully would have given you the full story long before now. The man has a mouth like a leaky bucket, big and incapable of holding anything back."

Jack chuckled. "You've got that right. He's an odd duck. Capable of taking secrets to the grave, but if he gets it into his head that telling a secret is in someone's best interest, he won't hesitate to spill it. I guess in his unfathomable wisdom, he must have thought this story was entirely yours to tell."

"Odd duck, indeed. As for why he didn't give you the low-down, I couldn't begin to guess. It's not like it's even an exciting story. Maybe we should wait for Griff to come back."

"I don't think the motivation behind that suggestion is as altruistic as it sounds. I think you'd best quit stalling, and spill."

***

ELLA LOOKED up as Griff returned, relieved at the opportunity to redirect the conversation. What was she thinking? How could she have admitted to Jack how much she used to love being caned, especially when she knew it would never be any kind of option, even if she were to wade back into the kinky pool. She sure didn't miss how his eyes lit up when she said it used to be her absolute favourite thing. She didn't think he could look any more excited. Then she mentioned her love of leather belts. She could almost hear the *ding ding ding, we have a winner* going off in

his head. She also didn't miss the quick flash disappointment he'd tried to hide when she took canes off the table.
Obviously, they were a bit of a favourite for at least one of
the pair.

Damn it, she should've kept her bloody mouth shut.
Even worse, she just kept getting hornier and hornier. As
terrifying as the thought of playing was for her, she kept
fixating on what it might be like to play with both of these
sexy men. She'd never had a threesome before, but that
didn't stop her from daydreaming about it and she had no
shortage of reading material featuring it. She could feast
on the *idea* of being the filling in a Griff and Jack sandwich
for months, the reality of it would probably provide her
with a life-time supply of wank-fodder. She mentally
smacked herself. *And exactly how did that going home with a
Domly stranger thing work out for you?* Yeah, she knew better
than most how the disaster of reality can be inversely
proportional to the ecstasy of fantasy.

She was so deep in her own head, she startled at Griff's
voice. "We're all set. Do we have a referee picked out?"

Jack patted her knee. "Ella would like Finn to ref, and
she'll talk to Mac about limits and such first." He looked
over to the spot where Mac and Finn had been playing and
then back at Griff. "It looks like they're done. Would you
like to go talk to Finn about it, or would you like to stay
here with Ella while I go?"

"I'll go. You two look comfortable and I'm already up.
Ella, I'll ask Mac to come and chat with you once she is
back to normal, okay? It might take some time, I think she
was pretty deep in sub-space there for a while."

"That would be great. Thank you." Ella lifted her hand toward her mouth, but Jack stopped it before it reached its destination.

"I know you need to think about what you'll want to talk to Mac about, but it would please me greatly if you could do it without damaging your body in the process."

Ella looked down at her hand. Embarrassed and ashamed, she tried to pull it from Jack's grip to hide it.

"Stop for a moment, love. I wasn't trying to embarrass you. It's a nervous habit, and one you probably wouldn't notice if someone didn't point it out to you. You're not the only person on the planet to do this, and you won't be the only one to overcome it. Don't worry, Griff and I will help you. I love to reward positive behaviour, so if you can get through the next thirty minutes without chewing on yourself, Griff and I will give you a third orgasm."

Ella did laugh then. She kept it quiet so she wouldn't disturb Wil and Hildy's scene, but the idea of a third orgasm, especially with the limits they had set, was ludicrous.

"Ah, a sceptic. I like that. Things are so much more fun when we have something to prove. Let me guess, most of the men you've been with were all talk and no orgasm."

Yeah, he had it in one. She didn't really want to admit it, but she thought confirming his suspicions would at least make them try harder, and maybe she would have a chance for at least one orgasm before she went home.

TWELVE

Ella had honestly thought Griff and Jack were blowing the same smoke regarding their sexual prowess as every other stud-wannabe she'd ever encountered. Of course, she was already wound up pretty tight by the time they were ready to start, but she still didn't think they'd be able to pull off a hat-trick with her fully clothed and no power tools.

They didn't touch her at all until they'd reached the spanking bench. Mac had promised her she wouldn't be restrained and her limits would be respected, but she was still apprehensive.

Jack took her by the hand and slowly pulled her towards him. He peppered the left side of her neck with tiny kisses as he wrapped his arms around her and his erection brushed against her belly. Oh boy, that was certainly worth bragging about.

Then Griff pressed behind her and nipped at her right earlobe. Wow, he wasn't lacking, either. Her tummy went all fluttery and her pussy felt like it was on fire. Her attempt to squeeze her legs together to give herself a little relief was thwarted when each man slipped a leg between hers.

Griff whispered in her ear, "Don't worry, honey, we'll take care of that for you, just like Jack promised. You just need to be patient."

Jack lifted his head and placed a soft kiss to her lips, then increased the pressure as he slid his tongue along the seam of her mouth.

"Let him in, baby." Griff's hot breath against her ear sent a new trickle of moisture into her already drenched panties.

She parted her lips and Jack traced them with the tip of his tongue before he caught her bottom lip between his teeth. He tugged gently and that flutter in her belly intensified. Jack cupped her cheek and kissed her once more before he pulled away. "Such a good girl. Now, up you get and lay on your back, sweetheart." Griff nipped her earlobe one more time, then helped her get settled on the bench.

They began stroking their hands all over her body, but never where she most desperately needed to feel their touch. Her breasts ached and her pussy spasmed with every heartbeat. Their fingers were barely a whisper, and for a moment, she found herself wishing her clothes away so she could feel those fingers on her skin. Then she remembered the level of disfigurement and was grateful for the fabric barrier.

She mentally gave her head a shake. Now wasn't the time to wallow in self-pity. She had two gorgeous men itching to do whatever it took to get her off three times without her having to remove one stitch of clothing. Even though she figured they had no chance of success, she missed being touched, and for now, she was perfectly happy to let them waste their time on her. Besides, if they did manage to deliver on their promise, so much the better. But damn, she wished they would just get on with it.

She was almost at her breaking point when heat engulfed both her nipples and sparks shot straight to her clit. Holy hell, she was already horny and now all she wanted was her pussy full of cock. She needed to keep her head in the game. These guys were dangerous. They were making her feel things she hadn't felt in a decade.

As Griff and Jack sucked on her nipples through the fabric of Mac's top, it occurred to Ella she'd need to get it cleaned before she could return it. A sharp nip on her right nipple and a hand slipping between her thighs reined in her wandering mind. Oh shit, she was primed and it wasn't going to take much at all to launch her into space. Fingers pressed hard against her clit and rubbed in all kinds of delicious ways as the suction on her nipples ebbed and flowed. She didn't bother trying to fight the looming orgasm. She wanted it more than her next breath. She was so close she wanted to lift her hips and reach for it, but those clever fingers saved her the trouble. They pressed harder and moved faster until she exploded.

They hadn't given her much time to recover from that first orgasm before they teased out the other two they'd promised and then added one more for the road. Yeah, these guys were dangerous.

GRIFF HAD BEEN silent for the whole drive home, and that had Jack more than a little worried. Working together to make Ella come had been a beautiful experience he was eager to build on, but what if Griff had changed his mind? He still harboured a soul-deep fear that Griff was going to abandon him for a woman, and he didn't know if he could survive it. Jack hated feeling in limbo, and as much as he wanted Griff to hurry up and say what was on his mind, pestering the man would only slow the process down. He left Griff to his own devices while he put his toy bag away and got ready for bed.

Jack was just about asleep when Griff finally slid into bed. He cuddled up behind him and nipped at his earlobe. Fuck, he would swear there was a direct line between his earlobe and his balls. "Hi." Griff continued to nibble and he wanted nothing more than to grind his ass against his lover's hard cock, but until Griff shared what was on his mind, sex of any kind was off the table. "Griff."

"Hush, I need you."

Dammit. He was screwed six ways from Sunday. It would be easier to go ahead and have sex. After that scene with Ella, he was certainly horny enough, but he needed to be sure this wasn't going to be the last fuck goodbye.

"Griff, stop. I know you've got something on your mind and you know I'm usually content to sit tight and wait until you're ready to talk, but I'm scared and I need to know if you're going to dump me so you can have Ella to yourself."

Griff pulled him in tight and kissed his neck. "Hell no. I was replaying that scene in my head and trying to figure out when we can play with her again, and how long we'll have to wait until we can get her naked and make her ours."

"Really?"

"Really. Jack, I hate that I've given you any reason to doubt my commitment to our relationship and it kills me that you still feel insecure. I meant what I said. If I can only have one person in my life, I choose you. I. Choose. You. Always. Do I want to see where things could go with Ella? Of course. But I'm not willing to risk what *is* for what *might be*. My heart belongs to you and it's yours to share or not. I love you."

God he felt like a selfish heel. "I'm sorry, babe."

"Don't. You can't help your feelings, and I don't ever want you to be sorry for them. Clear?"

"I'll try." And he would.

"Good enough. Now, speaking of selfish, I'm feeling pretty damned horny after that scene with Ella…"

Jack grinned and shimmied down the bed and took his lover's cock deep into his mouth.

# THIRTEEN

Ella ignored her phone again as she tried to read her smutty book. She wished they would all just stop pushing. She had successfully avoided sexual entanglements for the last ten years. It wasn't that difficult. She had three rules. Only date men she didn't find attractive; make it clear she wasn't a first date fuck; and make damn sure there was never a second date.

Now she was faced with not one, but two men who she wouldn't hesitate to break the rules for, and for her own safety, she needed to limit her time with them to final rehearsals only. No more letting Mac lure her to social functions where Griff and Jack would be.

She was smart enough to know Mac was manipulating her to attend, and she went along with it because they were a fun bunch of people to be around and she'd mistakenly thought she was strong enough to keep her libido out of the equation.

The knocking on the door was much more difficult to

ignore. Damn, she was relentless. Ella finally gave in when it became clear Mac wasn't leaving. She yanked the door open and stood there, saying nothing. She was angry and feeling more than a little regret for agreeing to pull that fucking piece out of mothballs. She wasn't going to make it easy for Mac to worm further into her life.

"Ella, are you okay? We haven't seen you in days and you haven't been answering your phone. I've been worried."

Fuck. The guilt card. "I'm fine, thanks. Just really busy."

"You don't look very fine."

"I'm just tired. I've got deadlines to meet and I've spent way too much time socialising." Not entirely a lie. She did have deadlines to meet, just not anytime soon. And she *had* been doing too much socialising.

"I don't buy that you're too busy to answer the fucking phone or return a fucking message for days on end."

Oh shit, Mac was getting mad. She needed to diffuse this fast. She couldn't handle Mac being angry at her. Time to figuratively roll over and bear the belly. "I'm sorry. I promise I'll return calls by the end of the day if I'm too busy to pick up. Okay?"

Mac gave her an indulgent smile. "Okay."

That wasn't so hard. Now she just had to get Mac to leave. "I'd invite you in for coffee, but I'm right in the middle of a break-through…" She trailed off, hoping Mac would take the hint. Again, not exactly a lie—her book *was* at a crucial point in the story.

"Sure thing. I'll let you get back to it." Mac's expression did nothing to hide her disappointment before she turned and headed down the steps.

Ella quietly shut the door before she let the first tears fall. She swiped at them with the back of her hand and headed for her bed. She was too upset to do anything, even read. She should have just continued to ignore the fucking door. She should have gone out for the day and left her phone at home.

She'd cried herself to sleep, and was a little disoriented when she woke up to a dark room and a persistent banging. All she wanted was her peaceful life back. As much she wanted to bury her head beneath her pillow and ignore the ruckus outside, it would be over much faster if she just sucked it up and answered the door.

She looked through the peephole and forced herself not to groan. She pasted on a bright smile and opened the door. "Mac, what can I do for you?"

Mac stood there with big pizza box, a loaded shopping bag, and a soft-sided cooler. "Girl's night."

Fuck. How the hell was she supposed to get out of this? The only way she knew how, lie. "Look, I've got a headache and I need to go back to bed."

"Too fucking bad, Ella. If you really do have a headache, go take something for it. Now move." Mac was wearing her dictator hat, and Ella had been around her enough to know the only option was to go with it, so she stepped back and let the woman in.

The moment she walked through the door, Mac set down her load and wrapped her arms around Ella, holding her tight. She tried to pull away, but Mac gave her another squeeze before letting her go. Mac picked up the pizza box and held it out. "Here, take this into the living room while I go grab the necessaries from the kitchen."

Ella set the box on the coffee table and lifted the lid. Hawaiian. Of course Mac would bring her favourite pizza —that was how she rolled. She closed the box and curled up in her favourite armchair while she wondered what other goodies Mac had up her sleeve. Girl's night, she'd said. Oh, how long it had been since she'd had one of those. Maybe it wouldn't be so bad.

Mac walked into the room carrying plates, a couple bottles of beer, and the shopping bag. She set everything on the table and rooted around in the bag for a moment before pulling out a handful of DVDs. "Chick-flicks. No girl's night is complete without them. Which one do you want to watch first?" She fanned the cases out so Ella could see the titles.

For the first time in what seemed like for ever, Ella smiled. Mac had brought musicals. "Let's go with *Some Like it Hot*, I could use the laughs."

"Excellent choice." Mac laid the rest of the cases on the table and inserted the film into the DVD player. She loaded a plate with pizza and sat on the sofa. She looked at Ella and flashed her irresistible grin as she patted the cushion beside her. "Come sit next to me. It'll be more fun. You'll have a better view of the TV and more important-ly," she waggled her eyebrows, "you'll be closer to the pizza."

Why did the woman have to make it impossible to stay grumpy? Ella grabbed a plate and a couple pieces of pizza before she parked herself on the sofa next to her friend. Yes, her friend. After so many weeks of fighting it, she finally accepted Mac's friendship. It was just easier. No, that wasn't entirely true. I *was* easier, but more than that, it felt so much better. She really did like Mac, and the idea of losing touch after the performance didn't sit well.

By the time they'd finished their third film, they'd also consumed most of the pizza, all the beer, and couple bags of potato chips. As the closing credits rolled, Mac grabbed a remote control in each hand and simultaneously hit the power button for the TV and the eject button for the DVD player.

"Hey, I was reading those," Ella complained.

Mac retrieved the DVD and popped it into its case before powering down the machine. "Tough titties, sunshine." She tossed the movie on top of the others sitting on the coffee table and returned to her spot on the sofa. "Okay, it's time to talk about your sub-drop."

Was the woman on crack? How could anyone possibly get sub-drop from a few little orgasms? "I was tired, is all."

"Sweetie, pizza, beer, and a few movies with a girl-friend does not magically make you un-tired. I was there, and you definitely hit a little subspace, and there's no doubt in my mind you've been suffering from sub-drop. And maybe a side of panic?"

"It was just post-orgasm buzz, not subspace, but I'll admit there may have been a little panic to go with the tired."

"Okay, we can call it tired, if that's what works for you, but whenever I think you're *tired,* I'm going to show up at your door with a pick-me-up. Deal?"

Ella sighed and gave in. "Deal." The sigh was more for show than how she really felt, but maybe Mac was on to something with this sub-drop business, because she definitely felt better now than she had in a couple of days. A trip to Google might be in order.

"Excellent. Now that you seem to be in better spirits, it's time for me to call Finn to come pick me up." Mac grabbed her phone off the coffee table and dialled.

## FOURTEEN

"A DATE."

Jack stopped scraping the reed he was making and looked up. "What are you on about?"

"I think we need to take Ella on a date," Griff said.

"Have you lost your mind? She doesn't even trust us in a group setting, what makes you think she'll agree to a date?"

Griff shrugged. "The worst that can happen is she'll make up some bullshit to avoid saying no, so what have we got to lose?"

"Babe, if we push her too hard, we're going to blow it and she's going to dive back into that hole of hers and never come out."

"Oh for fuck's sake, we've already messed up. We've been too hands-off with her. It should have been us helping her through her sub-drop. It was our responsibility, not Mac's."

"Okay, you make a good point," Jack conceded. "What do you have in mind?"

"Nothing specific. It's more along the lines of what I don't have in mind. Whatever it is, it can't set up the expectation of a post-date fuck or playtime. I think that's the most important thing."

"All right," Jack returned to scraping his reed as he continued, "what I'm hearing is, traditional date activities like dinner or a movie are out. Correct?" Griff nodded. "In that case, I think silly and fun might be in order. How about button pushing at the toy store."

"That definitely qualifies as silly and fun. Maybe go for ice cream after?"

"Yeah, I think ice cream is a great idea." Jack stopped scraping and held the reed up to the bright light on his work table. He flipped it back and forth a few times before placing it on the reed rack to dry.

"Just one thing…" Griff waited until Jack looked at him. "I think it's really important that this is a date—nothing more. No slipping in a little D/s, and for now, if we're alone with Ella, none of the good Dom, bad Dom shit. Getting her to trust us needs to be our first priority."

"Fair enough. However, I think we might have a better chance at success if we ask her in person at tomorrow's game night than we will if we phone her."

"Manipulative—but not unreasonably so. We should make our date on a weekday—there should be fewer kids in the store," Griff flashed a big grin, "and less competition for the buttons. I vote for Monday. I swear, that's the most un-date-like day of the week."

"Of course, it has nothing to do with it being the first

available weekday after tomorrow." Jack raised an eyebrow and Griff grinned back. "I wonder if there's any chance of her coming to the play party on Sunday."

"I'll call Mac and ask while you get your shit packed up. Then we can head to bed."

"Sounds like a plan."

Griff grabbed his phone and dialled. When Mac answered, he said, "Hang on, I'm going to put you on speaker." He hit the button and held the phone between himself and Jack. "There, now I won't have to repeat the whole conversation." Jack raised that damned eyebrow again, so Griff winked and suggestively licked his top lip before lowering his gaze to the rapidly growing bulge in Jack's jeans. Someone was getting lucky tonight.

"What's up, you two? I'm assuming you didn't hit mute by mistake."

"You're a cheeky wench. We were wondering whether Ella's going to be at your play party on Sunday."

Mac giggled. "And if she's not going to be there, you'd like me to do everything in my power to change her mind. Am I right?"

"Well…"

"Good grief. There are days when I wonder how any of you lot got your Dom cards. Yes, she's coming. You'll be happy to know, it didn't take any arm-twisting. Sub-drop aside, her experience with you two was positive enough for her to want to come again—in more ways than one, I'd imagine. We'll take that as a big win and move on."

"Thanks. Any advice for us?"

"Yeah, don't fucking let her suffer from sub-drop like that again."

"We won't."

"You'd better not, because rest assured, I will make it seriously suck to be you."

"Understood. We'll see you tomorrow."

"Goodnight."

Griff pushed the button to end the call and looked over at Jack. "Bedtime?"

"Yup. Last one there, bottoms." Jack jumped up and raced out of the room before Griff even had a chance to stand up.

"You're a dirty, rotten cheater, Jackson Riley," he yelled as he raced after his lover. Ah fuck it—it didn't matter whether he was bottom or top, he'd still get to come a time or two before they fell asleep.

---

Jack lazily stroked his hand up and down his condom-clad erection, slathering it in lube as he waited impatiently for Griff to arrive. Yeah, he'd cheated, but all's fair in love and fucking. Besides, they tended to bottom and top in fairly equal measure. He let his mind wander to Ella and how beautiful she'd looked when she came. He hoped they'd get to play with her on Sunday. He knew they were a long way from sex of any kind, let alone double-teaming her, but maybe fortune would smile on them and they would get to do a bit more than make her come fully clothed. His mouth watered at the idea of her naked and spread before him, her clit shyly peeking out ready to be sucked, tortured, and teased into submission.

"Care to share what's on your mind?"

Startled out of his daydream, Jack grinned and thrust his pelvis upward. "Later. Right now I'm more than ready to share what's in my fist. Hands on the wall, spread your legs, and brace yourself. I'm not feeling particularly gentle tonight."

As he stood behind Griff, Jack exposed his lover's asshole. Once he had his cock positioned at the entrance, he slipped his arms under Griff's and grabbed hold of his shoulders. "Relax. Deep breath, then let it out, babe." On the exhale, Jack pushed his hips forward with steady pressure as he pulled down on Griff's shoulders and bit into crook of his neck. The head of Jack's cock squeezed through the tight ring of muscle, and he savoured that fleeting moment of near pain before Griff's asshole relaxed and welcomed him in.

He didn't wait for Griff to adjust to him. As soon as he'd buried his entire length inside, he pulled out and slammed home. Griff moaned and rocked his hips, driving Jack to pump harder and faster. "Don't come," he growled in Griff's ear before he gave the lobe a sharp nip. A few more thrusts and he was there. He bit down hard on the crook of Griff's neck and groaned as he filled the condom.

He kissed the bite mark, then carefully pulled out. "Go sit on the bed, babe. As soon as I deal with this condom, I'm going to suck you dry.

## FIFTEEN

Ella tried to keep her jaw off the floor while her traitorous pussy soaked her panties as it throbbed and clenched with every beat of her racing heart. Wilson and Finn were spit-roasting Hildy while Mac teased her mercilessly with a vibrator. Ella felt a little sorry for poor Hildy having her mouth held open with a spider gag. Then again, considering the number, and apparent intensity of the orgasms she was having, chances were good its sole purpose was to prevent Finn's cock from being bitten off. Between sweat, tears, and drool, Hildy was soaked and looked like she'd had just about enough, but unless she dropped one of the balls she held in her hands or someone else called the scene, they'd all keep going. Wil gave Finn a discreet nod and they both increased the speed of their thrusts until Finn came in Hildy's mouth, followed by Wil in her pussy. The men quickly removed her restraints and Mac wrapped Hildy in a blanket before Wilson scooped her up and carried her to one of the sofas in the aftercare area.

Reading about it and watching videos on the internet could get her a little hot and bothered, but having a front row seat to live action had her downright horny. She wondered where Jack and Griff were. Although she hadn't outright asked Mac if they were coming, it was her understanding they never missed a party. She was a little surprised to find herself disappointed at their absence. Fuck. She needed to get her head on straight and her mind off Griff and Jack. They were dangerous. She should be relieved they hadn't come, not disappointed. She needed to focus her attention elsewhere.

She knew it would be a struggle to hide her envy, so she consciously avoided paying any attention to the sofa next to her where Wilson was taking care of Hildy. Instead, she turned her focus back to the play space where Mac was kneeling in front of Finn while he instructed her on the finer points of deep throating.

"Relax your throat and swallow. You can do it, love. Take it all for me just once, then we can move on to things that make you feel good."

Mac pulled back and dry heaved a couple of times before snapping at Finn. "Why don't *you* fucking relax and swallow while someone shoves something the size of a baseball bat down your fucking throat."

"Mac, that's enough. You're awfully close to crossing the line. Either take it for me or safeword."

"Fuck you."

"That didn't sound like your safeword. Wait there and

do not move." Finn went to the back of the room and grabbed some sort of slapper from the wall, then sat on a straight-backed chair in the middle of the room. He crooked his finger at Mac and spoke in a quiet voice that sent a shiver down Ella's back. "Come here, my love." Mac stalked across the room and stopped just beyond Finn's reach. He patted his knees. "Mac, " he warned, "over my knee or use your safeword."

She let out a big sigh. "You're being mean to me," she said as she settled over Finn's lap.

"Sweetheart, I know you meant that as an insult, and I'll try to take it as one, but as a sadist, it's kind of hard to take it as anything but flattery. Now, why are you being punished?"

"Because I was disrespectful."

"And what was your punishment last time?"

"Twenty strokes with your flute cleaning rod."

"Yes, and what is the punishment for repeat offences?"

"Double the last with whatever hitty-thing you choose."

"Indeed. This will be the last time we go with that particular punishment. It doesn't seem to be all that effective, and at this rate, I'm going to end up with a repetitive stress injury before the month is out. You'll have your forty with the viper slapper." He stroked the tip of it all over Mac's ass as he spoke. "This little baby is like a tawse except it's made of rubber instead of leather. No need to count, love. Colour?"

"I'm fucking green."

Finn immediately laid into her ass with rapid swats, but she didn't start screaming until the fourth strike. He stopped at the tenth, and when she was quiet, he checked in. "Colour, love?"

"Just fucking get it done. I'm green, you miserable fuck."

"Fair warning. I'm going to give you the next set of ten, then check in. If you're rude to me again, I'll do the remaining twenty without a break, but I'll drag them out to maximise your pain and discomfort."

Mac screamed, but remained stock still while Finn gave her ass another ten shots with that evil piece of rubber. Ella was fascinated. Mac wasn't tied down, she could use her safeword, yet she stayed put while Finn hurt her. When Mac mouthed off at Finn again during his next check in, Ella wanted to gag her or do something make her shut up before she got herself into shit so deep, she'd suffocate.

Two sets of feet appeared on the stairs and Ella's heart gave a little skip as Jack and Griff descended into the room. They caught her eye and grinned before silently crossing the room to join her. Griff sat to her left, his thigh tight against hers as he stretched his arm across the back of the couch. Jack sandwiched her in from the right. His arm joined Griff's behind her and he leaned in and whispered, "Sorry we're late, sweetie. A truck dumped its load half a block in front of us and we were stuck until they could clear a lane for alternating traffic. We did try calling Mac and Finn, but their phones kept going to voice-mail."

Damn, they made her want so badly and they hadn't done anything except sit next to her and explain their delay. She realised how much less concerned she was over Mac's well being now that her men had shown up. Fuck.

They weren't her men. They'd never be her men. She needed to think of them only as friends. Should be easy enough. Their plan to goof off together at the toy store tomorrow totally qualified as a friend activity. Besides, who on earth did date things on a Monday afternoon? She tried to ignore the warm bodies pressed against her as she turned her attention back to Mac and Finn.

"I guess you didn't plan on sitting comfortably for the next few days, love." Finn went back to work on Mac's ass, leaving a short pause between each strike. He maintained a steady rhythm and Mac continued to spout obscenities at him.

Then she screamed, "Red," and everything stopped. Finn immediately dropped the slapper to the floor and pulled her into his arms. He stroked her hair and murmured something into her ear. She nodded, and he carried her to the aftercare area, settling on the sofa next to Wilson and Hildy. Wilson covered Mac with her blanket and handed Finn a bottle of water.

Ella didn't know how to process Mac safewording. Part of her was relieved that it worked as intended and everything stopped, but part of her was freaked out that Finn would push so far she needed to safeword. Jack stroked her cheek and she turned to look at him, her eyes filled with unshed tears.

"It's okay, love. They have a healthy, loving relationship. Truth is, he's usually the one to call a scene, but occasionally, he'll push her to safeword. Look on it as reaffirming their trust in each other. He trusts her to use her safeword appropriately, and she trusts him to stop when she does. I know you had a bad experience, so I get that us saying the right words doesn't mean shit to you right now, but maybe there will come a time when you'll be able to reconcile our words with our actions and even feel safe enough to explore a relationship with us."

Ella shook her head. A relationship meant at some point, they'd expect to hear the whole sordid tale of what happened that night. She had enough trouble with that shit popping into her head unannounced, there was no way she was going to send it an engraved invitation. However, she did think Jack had a valid point on the words versus actions thing. After all the time she'd spent with the group in general, and Griff and Jack in particular, their behaviour had always been consistent with their words. Besides, deep in her soul, she knew Sully would never spend any of his precious time with people who weren't genuine. Sadly, that knowledge did nothing to alleviate her nagging doubt. She made a show of checking her watch. "I should get going."

"Really?" Griff asked. She turned to face him and he continued. "Do you really mean you should be going, or do you mean you're scared and you should be avoiding any possibility of conflict?"

She pressed her lips together as she tried to formulate a believable answer.

Jack gave her thigh a gentle squeeze. "The only right answer is the truth, Ella. Try it. The world won't explode if you say something you think we won't like."

Her heart hammered in her chest and her head felt wonky. She couldn't do this.

"Get her a glass of water, would you, Griff?"

"Sure thing."

She felt the sofa shift as Griff stood, and Jack pulled her in close, stroking her hair and peppering the top of her head with tiny kisses. "It's going to be fine, sweetheart. I promise. Like I told you before, the truth always gets rewards."

It was their fucking rewards that had got her into this mess. Four fucking orgasms and she was ready to throw away her rules and risk the safety they afforded. She weighed her options. Her usual tactics failed miserably with this pair. Most people weren't inclined to call bullshit when she pulled even the flimsiest excuse out of her ass, but these two didn't hesitate. Complete avoidance got her girl's night with Mac and a lecture on sub-drop. Unfortunately, she was down to one last, drastic option. She gave it a pretty good chance of succeeding, but she'd have to make herself vulnerable.

---

GRIFF SNUGGLED tight against Jack's side with his ear right over Jack's heart, but still felt like he couldn't get close enough. Jack stroked his face and kissed the top of his head. He'd managed to stay tough all night, but now he was safe in his lover's arms, and he couldn't control his tears. While the scene did end in multiple orgasms for Ella, it had been an emotional cluster-fuck of epic proportions for Jack and him.

"It'll be fine, babe. You'll see."

"How can you say that? You saw what that psycho-fuck did to her," Griff said through his sniffles.

"Yes, I did. I also saw how she used it to get us to give up on her. Think about that for a minute. Do you think she would have exposed herself like that if she weren't running out of ways to push us away?"

"Well, I guess not, but—"

"But nothing. The only thing that went totally wrong with that scene was Ella thinking we were shallow enough to walk out on her once we saw what that wasted sperm did to her. How about we talk about all the right from that scene? And I've gotta tell ya, naked Ella eclipsed pretty much everything for me. Yeah, she's marked up some, but damn, she's got a gorgeous shape and she sure does taste good."

Griff smiled as he remembered how much he enjoyed licking and sucking at her juicy pussy. "Mmm. True. You're falling for her pretty hard, aren't you?"

"Not any harder than you are, babe."

"I guess that means we'll have to step up our game."

"Maybe. But I'm not sure she has anything left in her arsenal to fight us with. I suspect her putting her scars on display like that was her big gun. She figured we would take one look and run away screaming. She was wrong. All we need to do is make her understand we think she's beautiful and it has nothing to do with her skin."

"Is that all?" Griff snorted.

"Yup, and we get another chance to do exactly that tomorrow. In the meantime, I have other business to attend to."

Jack wiggled his way down the bed and Griff moaned as he felt the warm, wet tongue swirl around the head of his cock. He lifted his hips to get more, but Jack pinned them to the bed before swallowing him down in a long, slow slide. Oh boy, it looked like it was going to be one of those nights where Jack would tease him mercilessly for hours before making him come. He loved it when Jack was in that mood.

## SIXTEEN

Ella paced up and down the length of her living room. Her entire week had gone to shit in a handbag and she couldn't believe how badly she'd fucked everything up. Jack and Griff should have either fucked off without a backward glance, or given her the pity stare. She would have been fine with either option. Then it would have been easy for her to write them off and she could get back to the life she was comfortable with.

Now she was fresh out of options and she didn't know what to do. They'd held her to her commitment on Monday afternoon, and as much as she didn't want to have fun, she'd had a fucking blast.

They'd wandered up and down the aisles of the big chain toy store and pushed buttons on every electronic toy they encountered. Then they'd gone to the video game department and tried out all the consoles. She'd never considered owning one before, but another game or two and she might be convinced to buy herself one of those bad boys.

She smiled as she remembered their trip to the gelato shop afterwards. It was the first time she'd ever been there, and holy shit, she'd never seen so many different flavours of ice cream in her life. They ranged from regular old vanilla and chocolate to the outrageously bizarre, and her men—fuck, there she went with that *her men* business again—convinced her to sample at least three strange flavours of their choosing. They started her off with garlic. It wasn't bad, but she wouldn't want a whole cone of it. She even tried the curry flavour, but when Jack held out the spoon with wasabi on it, she baulked. She just couldn't do it. She started to panic when she couldn't come up with a way to avoid it.

Then Griff leaned down and whispered in her ear. "If you really can't do it, just call red, sweetheart. No harm, no foul."

She'd looked at the ice cream and thought about why she always ordered her sushi with no wasabi. She took a deep breath, and then another before she rose up on her toes and whispered, "Red," into Griff's ear.

The world hadn't exploded.

"Such a good girl," Griff said as he pulled her into his arms. "That wasn't so bad, was it?"

She shook her head. He cupped her chin, tipped her face up, and placed a gentle kiss on her lips. "There you go then. Red is the new no."

Jack shot her a big grin and licked the offending wasabi ice cream off the spoon with a dramatic flourish. Then they'd bought her a homemade waffle-cone filled with three scoops of the most amazing chocolate ice cream she'd ever tasted.

She looked at the clock, they'd be here any minute. She cursed herself for what must have been the hundredth time since agreeing to this. She had to be nuts. A date? An honest to goodness, dinner and a movie date? Then it hit her. This was her out. They'd kept her so off balance lately, she hadn't connected the dots. This was a first date. She only did first dates. Okay, she'd messed up on the rule about only dating unfortunate looking men, but as long as she kept rules two and three, she should be able to send them packing at the end of the evening.

JACK STRUGGLED to hold back the laugh, and he carefully avoided catching Griff's eye for fear they'd both lose it as Ella stood at her front door and politely explained her two unbreakable rules for dating. His sadistic side was looking forward to her reaction when he pointed out she was actually down to one unbreakable rule. His softer side... well, his softer side had a front row seat and a big bag of popcorn.

"Sweetie, what do you consider a date?"

"What we just did. Dinner and a movie." She paused and added, "I guess you could include going to a café or a pub."

"So, would it be fair to say your interpretation of a date is any outing involving food or drink?"

"I suppose..." She trailed off.

Nope, there was no mistaking her light bulb moment and she made the cutest little frown when it hit.

He reached out and gently stroked her cheek. "It's okay, sweetie. We've reached a fork in the road, and now it's time for you to decide which route you're going to take. I need you to understand, we're here for you and we'll keep you safe, whichever route you take. As much as we'd love to explore an intimate, kinky relationship with you, we're your friends first and always.

"You've got a lot to think about. To help you with your decision, Griff and I will send you our check-lists. Before you read them, fill one out of your own, then compare them. Maybe that will help you with your decision." Jack leaned down and pressed a gentle kiss on Ella's lips. "We're going to head home. We'll give you all the time you need to do your thinking, but that doesn't mean we're going to leave you alone."

Jack stepped aside, making room for Griff, who cupped Ella's chin and gave her a long, lingering kiss. Mildly irritated, he tapped Griff's shoulder. "Enough, studly. It's time for us to go home."

After breaking the kiss, Griff stared into Ella's eyes as he brushed his thumbs over her cheekbones. "Have a good sleep, sweetheart. Jack and I will be in touch. Now go inside and lock the door. We won't leave until you do."

She turned and entered the house, giving the men a small wave before closing the door. Once they heard the deadbolt slide home, they headed down the steps. Jack pointed the remote and pressed the unlock button.

They climbed into the car, and as he fastened his seat belt, Griff said, "Well, that went better than I feared."

Jack turned the key in the ignition, then pulled out into the street. "It did. There's still a lot of work ahead of us, though. I'm glad we filled out new check-lists yesterday. I'm hoping Ella will look on it as more proof of our sincerity than us trying to convince her we're being what we think she wants."

"Regardless of the Ella factor, I noticed we both had a few changes from when we last did them."

Jack chuckled. "Yeah. I'm still trying to figure out if that's a good thing, or a bad thing."

"If everyone involved is on board, does it matter?"

"Well, no."

"There you are then. As with many things in life, our tastes evolve, and as long as we're having a good time, I'm not going to sweat it. Speaking of a good time…" Griff unfastened Jack's trousers and extracted his cock.

Jack had been hard pretty much since they'd picked Ella up for their date. "If you're not planning to blow me, you'd best put that right back where you found it. I'm on a hair trigger, and if I end up spraying the interior of my car with spunk, you'll be the one cleaning it up."

"I was going to, but it's probably safer if I hold off until we get home. I will, however, leave your cock out where I can enjoy it. Besides, if you are that close, I don't want to be stuck cleaning your car just because I tried to cram your dick back in your trousers."

"You are such a fucking tease. I'm tempted to pull over and take care of business myself, and still make you clean up, because if you hadn't pulled my cock out in the first place, I wouldn't be in this predicament."

"You won't. I know you'd much rather come down my throat than redecorate the interior of your car."

"You're right, I would," Jack admitted. "In fact, I'm going to fuck your throat raw tonight, babe."

Griff unzipped his own trousers and pulled out his raging hard-on. "Fair enough, but that means I get your ass, and *gentle* sure as fuck isn't in my vocabulary right now."

"Sounds good to me." Jack checked the speedometer and backed off the accelerator a little. He did not need to get pulled over by the cops for speeding while he and Griff both had their dicks out, ready for action. He tried to focus on the road instead of the cock being stroked in his peripheral vision. Thank fuck they were only a few blocks from home, because, damn, that man knew how to torment.

They arrived home a few minutes later, and they raced into the house, cocks bobbing in the breeze. Once they were safely inside, Griff dropped to his knees and tugged Jack's trousers down to his thighs. He looked up and smiled before sliding his mouth all the way down on Jack's cock.

ELLA LEANED against the door and let herself slide down it. This was not going according to plan at all. They were supposed to run the other way, not try harder to get close. Maybe the check-lists were the answer. If they were totally incompatible, then they'd leave her alone. But what if they weren't?

Somewhere between the tell-tale beep of the car

remote and the roar of the engine, the loneliness set in. It was an odd thing, that soul-sucking loneliness. It was like a black hole opened in her chest whenever Griff and Jack left, devouring all the peace and contentment she felt when she was with them. They'd flipped her world on its side these past weeks, and worse, she wasn't sure she hated it.

She picked herself up off the floor and debated whether she wanted tea or something stronger before she went in search of a check-list to fill out. She was awfully tempted to hold off until she'd had a chance to go over Griff and Jack's lists, but it felt disrespectful—too much like cheating. Besides, deep down, she wanted a real sense of their compatibility.

Tea lost, and she sat on the sofa with her laptop and a beer. She did a search for check-lists and was boggled by the sheer number of results that came back. How the fuck was she supposed pick from these. What if she picked the wrong one? She didn't want to compare beer to wine.

A quick phone call to Mac and her problem was solved. She disconnected the call and started obsessively clicking the refresh button as she waited for the arrival of the email with the promised check-list attached. She took a swig of beer from the bottle, hoping that would speed things up. It didn't. She checked her watch and felt silly. It hadn't even been five minutes since she and Mac had spoken. Staring at the screen wasn't going to make things happen any faster. It would be better to do this business while all comfy, so she picked up her laptop and beer and headed to the bedroom.

By the time she'd changed into her pyjamas and settled

into bed with her laptop, Mac's email had arrived. Why was her heart trying to beat its way out of her chest? She closed her eyes for a moment, then she clicked on the attachment and waited for it to load and open.

Holy shit. She didn't remember check-lists being this long and involved back in the day. As she scanned through the document, she had to keep reminding herself that not everyone had the same taste in food, clothes, or kink, and it was not her place to judge. With such a wide-ranging assortment, she figured chances were pretty good that there would be stuff Griff and Jack were into that she'd totally red-light on and she found that thought disappointing.

She clicked to print the document, chugged the rest of her beer, and popped off to the bathroom to pee and brush her teeth. She grabbed the pages off the printer on her way back to bed. She had a drawer full of pens and pencils in a cup on her nightstand and after silently weighing the decisiveness of pen against the versatility of pencil, she settled on her favourite green pen—she was being bold. Why not? It wasn't like she couldn't print off another copy and change her answers.

As she made her way through the list, she hadn't expected to have such strong feelings. Not just about things she felt positive and negative about for herself, but how much she wanted Griff and Jack to feel the same way about these things as she did. She wondered how long they would make her wait before they sent her their check-lists.

It took far longer for her to get through the document than she'd anticipated, and when she was finally done, she knew she should turn out the light and go right to sleep, but curiosity and impatience won out and she checked her email one last time. Nothing. Just as well. She was wound up enough with possibilities without having probabilities swimming around in her head, too.

She already knew they could play her body like a Mozart concerto and heaven help her, she adored it. They'd pulled her so far out of her head, for a short time she'd even felt beautiful. She had forgotten how that felt and she had immediately wanted to bury it away. It was too unfamiliar and scary. Now she'd had some time to let it all percolate, she wanted more.

She lay in the dark, remembering the feel of their hands on her bare skin. How they'd eagerly sought it out. How there had been no hesitation after she'd stripped. They'd both grinned like they'd hit the jackpot instead of the booby-prize. Hell, it was days later and they still looked at her like she was the only woman in the world. She'd stopped playing the *what if* game years ago, but the way things had been going, especially this past week, she was tempted to let herself dream. Just a little.

## SEVENTEEN

Ella sat across the table from Jack and Griff and concentrated on not throwing up. How had she gone from a life of vanilla sex for one to negotiating kinky sex for three? She studied the papers she held in her hands while her pussy developed a slow-leak in her panties. Griff and Jack had collated the check-list data for all three of them into an easy to read spread-sheet. Just one more thing to add to the compatibility column.

When she'd received their check-lists, she'd done exactly the same thing, apparently with the same results. It had to be a trick of some kind—there was no way their likes and dislikes could be so closely aligned. Except, completing that list was the first time she'd let her kinky self free in years and if *she* didn't know what she was into anymore, how could anyone else?

The sounds floating up from Finn and Mac's playroom were strangely comforting. As scary as it was to have *the talk* with Griff and Jack, doing it where others were around felt that little bit safer. They'd told her to come prepared to spend the night. She probably shouldn't have, but it didn't hurt to have options. Between the flirty emails and suggestive comments over the phone, those sneaky fuckers had kept her simmering for days.

"Ella?"

She turned her attention to Griff. His brow was slightly furrowed, but he had a twinkle in his eye. "Yes?"

"Any questions?"

"No, I don't think so." Shit, she was really going to do this. She was going to get down and kinky with two men. At the same time. Yeah, she'd been naked while they'd both made her come until she thought her clit might expire from exhaustion, but she'd only been on the receiving end, and didn't consider it to be even in the same universe as the three of them being naked and participating equally. Well, not exactly equally given any threesome between them would always consist of two Doms and a sub.

Griff reached across the table and stroked her hand. "Fair enough. We'd like to start by setting the ground-rules. We'll both be keeping a close eye on you, as will the others, I suspect, and anyone one of us can, and will stop the action if it looks like you're struggling. However, if at any point you don't feel a bright and cheery green, you need to safeword. Yellow will do if you don't want to call a complete halt to the action, but if you feel so much as pink, you'd best call red. Understood?"

"Understood." More than understood. Fuck, she would swear these guys had a direct line of communication to her clit because that little display of domliness sure turned on the tap, and that leak was no longer slow.

"Good girl. We've got a very easy scene planned for tonight. We're going to take things slow, and for now, we'll tell you up front what to expect. We won't give you the details—we don't want to spoil all the surprises—but we will give you a fair idea what's in store. If you think you're going to have any issues, let us know, and we'll talk it through and figure it out. Okay?"

"Okay."

"Excellent. All we're planning to do in the playroom tonight is get half-naked and do some touching. Is that something you're willing to try?"

Touching? She could do touching. Damn, she'd been wanting to touch for ages. Taste, too. "Yeah."

"Remember, we're only asking you to try, sweetheart. If you're ready, then let's get moving."

They all stood, and Griff joined her on the other side of the table. He took her hand in his and brought it to his lips. "Come with me. Jack will join us shortly."

Griff led her down the stairs and she stopped abruptly at the bottom. Hildy was trussed up in neon-green rope and suspended from an overhead beam in the middle of the room. Griff wrapped his arms around Ella from behind and pulled her in tight as he kissed her neck.

She startled, and before she had a chance to move, Griff whispered in her ear. "We're in no hurry. We can watch from here for a bit."

Ella was still getting used to seeing the sexcapades Wil and Hildy got up to with Mac and Finn, and this time was no different. Mac was fucking Hildy's cunt with a strap-on, and every time Mac withdrew, Finn smacked her ass with his belt. Meanwhile, Wilson was at Hildy's head, plumbing the depths of Hildy's throat with his cock.

The more she watched, the more impatient she became for her own playtime to start. A second pair of arms surrounded her waist and hugged her closer. Jack. For him to have that kind of hold on her, he had to be pressed hard against Griff's back and judging from increased twitching, the erection crushed against her back wasn't all for her. Her belly fluttered and she squeezed her thighs together. This was the first time she'd actually encountered Jack and Griff interacting intimately with each other and it shot her straight from a little horny to do-me-now. The reality of the these two men together touched a side of her sexuality she hadn't been aware of. Until that moment, she hadn't really connected with the hot factor of man-on-man love. Sure, she was part of the mix, but up until that moment, they'd both focused all their attention on her and none on each other.

"Time to move, sweetness," Griff whispered in her ear. He gave her another kiss on her neck, then all the hands around her waist were gone. Griff took hold of her hips and gently pushed her towards the aftercare area. She stole a backwards look and saw Jack had a similar hold on Griff. Damn, she was a fucking puddle. They stopped in front of the fainting couch and Griff turned her around.

She looked up into those two gorgeous faces—all smiles and twinkling eyes—and her heart stalled. Love? She gave her head a mental shake. Maybe, but it wasn't for her. It couldn't be. It had to be for each other and she was just misreading their expressions. A little wishing couldn't hurt, though.

Jack reached out and stroked her cheek. "Time to get started. Colour?"

It took Ella a few seconds to get her head back in the game, but she was definitely in. "Green."

"Good girl. Take Griff's shirt off, please."

She didn't bother hiding the grin. She'd been dying to see what these guys were packing under their clothes for far too long. She grabbed the hem of Griff's t-shirt and pulled it up. He leaned forward and she whipped the shirt the rest of the way off.

"Slow down, sweetness, we've got all the time in the world." Griff kissed the tip of her nose and stepped in behind her. She loved the feel of a man's body against her back and his cock nestled in the crack of her ass. "Jack's shirt next. I think I'll give you a hand. You seem a little too eager." He clasped her wrists and guided her hands to the top button of Jack's shirt. She unfastened it and Griff used her hands to reveal the first glimpse of Jack's chest. She tried to touch the naked skin, but Griff moved her hands to the next button.

"Do only as you're told, love. I never said anything about touching." Griff nibbled at her ear as she continued to undo the buttons. By the time she'd got to the last two, she was fresh out of patience. She leaned forward, intending to lick Jack's nipple, but Griff gave her ear a sharp nip and his grip on her tightened before she could get close enough.

"Licking counts as touching. Don't worry, sweetness, you'll get your chance. I promise." He loosened his hold on her as he shifted her hands, and together they finished with the buttons. Griff released her wrists. "Slide it off slowly, then you can lick *one* nipple."

She reached up and grasped the edges of the shirt and eased them over Jack's shoulders. As the fabric skimmed down his arms, Ella leaned in and brushed the tip of her tongue over Jack's left nipple. His small groan made her pussy throb.

She pulled off his shirt and let it fall to the floor, but before she could get her hands on his chest, Jack grasped them and lifted them above her head. "Don't move." He released her hands and leaned in and kissed her. His tongue found its way between her lips and she immediately began to tease and suckle it. Her belly flip-flopped as she thought about doing exactly this to his cock.

Griff slipped his hands under her shirt and slid it up her body. She shivered. His fingers trailed along her skin leaving goosebumps in their wake. She was so turned on, she wanted to reach down between her legs and fix the problem. After so many years of being entirely responsible for her own orgasms, it felt strange not to give in to her urges whenever they arose. Jack broke the kiss and Griff tugged the garment free.

Jack scooped her into his arms. "You are such a good girl." He carried her to the fainting couch and sat, settling her into his lap. She rested her cheek on his shoulder and closed her eyes. His bare skin against hers made her want. Not just the orgasms her men—yes, they were definitely her men—were guaranteed to deliver. No, she wanted so much more than physical pleasure. She wanted to be connected—to *feel*. She wanted love.

A few minutes later, she felt the couch shift with Griff's

weight as he sat next to them. Jack leaned in, taking Ella with him. Griff's arms closed around them, and being safely tucked in the middle, Ella felt at peace.

"Not done yet, sweetness." Griff kissed Ella and Jack, then released them from his embrace. "We're going to play a guessing game. Every correctly guessed item is an orgasm for you. Every time you incorrectly guess an item, you lose an orgasm."

"What happens if I end up getting more wrong than I get right?"

"I'm so glad you asked. If you're behind by the time we get to the last item, your answer will determine whether you get an orgasm tonight or not. When I tell you to, you are going to turn around so you're facing Jack. Knees either side of his legs, arms around his neck, and eyes on him. Once you're in position, you are not to move. You may only speak to guess what the object is or to safeword. Understood?"

"Yes."

"Good girl. Time to play."

She wasn't normally a cheat, but she was feeling off balance, so she thought she'd sneak a peek at the things she would need to identify while she re-positioned herself. Jack thwarted that plan. First he guided her in the wrong direction, then he shifted until he was reclining. She wanted to rub up and down the erection nestled hard against her clit, and if he hadn't held her hips so tightly, she might have given in to temptation.

"Soon, baby," Jack whispered in her ear. "We'll get there, I promise, but we've got some games to play first. Green if you're ready, yellow if you're not."

"I'm green."

"Good girl. Let's get started, Griff."

The soft tickle at the base of her neck was easy. "Feather?"

"Well done. The girl wins an orgasm." Ella giggled at the silliness in Griff's voice. "Ready for the next one, sweetie? A quick reminder, green for yes, Yellow for no."

"Mmm, green."

With so many soft tails trailing down her back, the next one was just as easy. "Flogger."

"Excellent. You're up to two orgasms. Shall we continue?"

Ella nodded and Jack nipped her earlobe. "We need a colour, love."

"Still green."

"On we go, then."

The next thing to touch her was trickier. It was wide, smooth, and its coolness made her shiver as travelled down her back. It was hard rather than flexible, so she took a wild guess. "Some kind of paddle?"

"Clever girl. The score is Ella three, Jack and Griff, nil. We're down to the last two, so even if you guess wrong on both, you're still guaranteed to get one orgasm. Ready?"

"Green."

"I love how obedient you are. I think we might have to speed things up a bit, though, because Jack looks like he's just about at his limit."

"Shut up and get on with it," Jack growled. His cock flexed against Ella's clit and she was aching to pull it out of his jeans, slide her panties aside, and impale herself.

Griff chuckled. "Patience, you two. Almost done."

The final two items were impossible for Ella to recognise. She hadn't expected kitchen utensils so it was little wonder she got the miniature silicon spatula wrong. The last one, however, was a complete shock. She recognised the rhythm from *Rhapsody in Black and Blue* as the instruments bounced gently up and down her back, loosening the tight muscles. After all the agony she'd experienced from canes that horrible night, she would never have imagined they could bring pleasure. Even more unimaginable? She wanted more.

"Another day, sweetheart." Griff leaned in and kissed her cheek. "You've earned yourself one orgasm, and we're going to give you a chance to earn a second."

"How do I do that?"

"You need to put the toys away. I'll come with you to show you where they all live, but you'll have to do the work. Are you up to that?"

She turned her head to see the toys Griff had used lined up behind her on Jack's legs.

The canes kept drawing her attention. Could she touch them?

She frantically shook her head and Jack pulled in and hugged her tight and asked, "Can you give me a colour?"

Her mind screamed the childhood tongue-twister, red leather, yellow leather, over and over.

"Okay, baby, I'm going to give you yes or no questions, and you can nod or shake your head. Okay?" Ella nodded. "Good girl. Can you do the job if it doesn't include the canes?"

No canes? No problem. She nodded again and Jack kissed the top of her head.

"All right, then. Griff will take care of the canes, and you can do the rest. When you're done, you'll come back here for your aftercare. Are you green?"

"Green."

"You're our good girl. Off you go, then."

By the time Ella had climbed off Jack, Griff had already removed the canes. She gathered up the remaining toys and followed Griff.

The others had finished playing, and Hildy and Mac were snuggled up in Wil and Finn's laps. Mac gave an exaggerated wink and a big grin as Ella walked past. Bugger, if that woman didn't keep finding ways to make her feel at ease.

When she and Griff reached the other side of the room, he pointed to where she should put the paddle. By the time she'd turned back to face him for directions on where to put the flogger, his hands were empty. He shot her that cheeky grin of his, and she smiled back. It was that moment she realised just how well they understood her. They knew just how hard to push, and when to back off.

Yeah, canes were a hard limit under impact play and she should probably be pissed because technically, they'd violated that limit. But she had marked massage as something she really loves, and damned if those men hadn't used that as a loophole. And she was oddly okay with that.

"Come on, sweetness." Griff took her by the hand and led her back to Jack, who wrapped her in the blanket he was holding.

He pulled her back into his lap as he sat down and

Griff handed her some chocolate as he seated himself next to them.

"We're going to spend the night here. So are Wilson and Hildy, although, I suspect they won't be using a guest room, and I highly doubt there will be much sleeping going on. Jack and I would love it if you would spend the night with us. No pressure. You can participate as much or as little as you like. You get your orgasms regardless. If you choose to spend the night, we'll take care of you once we go to bed. If you choose not to stay, then we'll make you come here before we take you home."

The breeding ball of snakes currently residing in the pit of her stomach screamed at her to *go home* before she gets herself killed this time! But Mr. Spock logic kept comparing situations and pointing out these men were nothing like the pretty boy, and if she stayed, it would be nothing like the horrible night. She wanted to go to Mac for reassurance, but it was time to stand on her own feet.

"Yes, I'll stay."

Griff reached around and hugged her and Jack tight. "Now's as good a bedtime as any, I think."

ELLA LAY NAKED on top of the bed while she watched Jack and Griff finish stripping each other. It was scorching-hot having the two of them remove what was left of her clothing, but watching them take care of each other was off the charts. She was dying to play with herself, but once they'd got her completely stripped, they'd positioned her arms above her head and her legs spread wide, then ordered her not to move.

Holy shit, mental bondage did it for her in a way that physical bondage never had. Back before the horrible night, she'd been into being tied up, big-time. But the depth of submission she felt from maintaining a position simply because she was told to, was so much deeper and more satisfying than anything she'd felt from being physically restrained.

"Look at our good girl, Griff. Her clit is pulsing. She's so horny, I bet she's dying to slide a finger or two inside that sweet pussy of hers. What do you think, should we let her play with herself?"

"Maybe later. I see that glistening pussy and all I want to do is feast on it. It's been too long since I've tasted our girl. I think she should have some choices, though." Griff sat on the edge of the bed and teased her nipple with his finger. "So, sweetness, would you rather suck Jack's cock or have him suck mine while I'm dining on you?"

Or? What did he mean, or? "I'd like all of the above."

A look passed between Griff and Jack, then they both smiled wide. "All of the above it is, then. On your side, love."

Ella didn't waste any time getting herself into position. Her mouth was watering and she was anxious for her first taste of Jack. She didn't have long to wait before Jack's cock bumped against her lips. She opened and swiped at the drop of liquid at the tip.

Griff re-positioned her legs before he slid his tongue deep inside her. That man had skills—and a tongue rivalling that of Gene Simmons probably didn't hurt, either.

She focused on the cock in front of her as best she could. She was so out of practice, but if his moans and gyrating pelvis were any indication, Jack didn't seem too concerned. She swirled her tongue around the head before sliding it into her mouth. She thought back to Hildy swallowing Wil's cock to the root earlier. Nope, she was definitely too out of practice for that, but she did take him as deep as she dared without risking her gag reflex. She pulled back and gently suckled at the tip, hoping she might get a glimpse Griff's cock in Jack's mouth before she slid down on him again. There were too many body parts blocking her view, so she returned her attention to the cock in her mouth.

She'd missed this so much. She cupped Jack's balls and squeezed gently with one hand while she worked the lower part of his shaft with the other. She kept taking him as deep as she dared, moving a little faster each time. She could feel him getting close, and in a split second, she knew she'd happily swallow whatever he gave her. She was just about to go to town when Jack withdrew completely.

She only had a moment to care before Jack's mouth engulfed her nipple. He sucked long and hard while Griff sucked her clit with the same rhythm and intensity. Two fingers slid inside, then a third. She was almost there.

Jack released her nipple with a pop and pushed her onto her back. He kissed her hard, sliding his tongue in and tangling it with hers. He cupped her her breasts in his hands and gently squeezed her nipples with his thumbs and forefingers.

She tried to contain her frustration as Griff reduced the suction on her clit. He gave her only enough to keep her on edge, but not enough to go over. She tilted her pelvis up, trying to get more pressure on her clit, but Griff pulled away and lifted his head.

The sharp nip Jack gave her earlobe made her flinch and stop mid-protest. "No whining. You only get what we give you. If you try to take more, we'll give you less." She wasn't quite sure if that nipping thing he kept doing was punishment or not. He always seemed to get it to a point where it hurt, but still managed to make her tingle in all the right places.

"Time for more choices, sweetie," Griff said. "The first decision you need to make is how you get your first orgasm. Tongue or cock?"

It had been so long since she'd had a cock inside her, and as wonderful as Jack and Griff's tongues and fingers felt, she wanted to feel full. "Cock, please."

"Since I got the first taste of you with my tongue, it's only fair for Jack to get first taste of you with his cock. Are you ready for your next choice?"

"Yes." But she wasn't really. She didn't want to make any more choices, she just wanted to get fucked, and she was tired of waiting.

"Good girl. This is the last decision you'll have to make tonight, Do you want to suck my cock while Jack fucks you, or do you want me to fuck Jack while he fucks you?"

Holy shit. Did he really just ask that? Fuck it. This might be her only opportunity to go big before going home and she was not going to miss out. Her heart pounded and her vision started to darken from the edges, but she refused to let the tendrils of panic take over. "I want you to fuck Jack."

Both men smiled wide and Jack said, "You get the supplies, I want to have a taste of our girl first."

Griff rose from his spot between Ella's legs and Jack took his place. His tongue wasn't as long as Griff's, but it was every bit as talented. Seriously, flutter-tonguing had to be the number one reason to date a wind or brass musician. Then Jack provided the reason why one should never discount the thumb dexterity of a bassoonist.

Just as she was getting close to coming, Jack backed off. "Soon, baby. Remember, you're the one who chose orgasm by cock. You stay put while Griff and I suit up."

"Can't I help?" Damn, she wanted to touch.

"Not this time, love. You just stay put and watch."

Okay, watching was *almost* as good as touching. And he'd said not *this* time, she took that to mean a next time was possible and let herself dream a little more.

She tried not to squirm as she watched Griff lay a bottle of lube on the bed and hand Jack a condom. This was really happening. After he unfurled a condom over Griff's erection, Jack squirted a big dollop of lube in his palm and slathered it all over Griff's cock. Ella wished it was her hand gliding up and down the slippery shaft.

Griff moaned and grabbed Jack's wrist. "Enough."

"Oh no," Ella interrupted, "carry on, that's hotter than hell"

"Don't you worry, Ms. Ella," Griff said as he unrolled a condom over Jack's cock, "you're going to get plenty of opportunities to indulge your voyeuristic urges, but right now, we've got other plans for you."

Jack held her gaze as he knelt between her legs and slid one, then two fingers inside her. She wanted to rock against them, but she would be a good girl. He gently pumped his fingers in and out before adding a third. He held his fingers still while his thumb worked its magic on her clit.

He continued to tease her, and when she was on the verge of coming, he withdrew his hand. Just as she was beginning to re-think her position on being a good girl, she felt the tip of Jack's cock at her entrance.

He leaned forward so their chests touched, resting his weight on his forearms. "We're going slow and easy this time, sweetie, but fair warning, hard and fast is definitely in our future."

Ella closed her eyes and clung to his words. *This time*, and *our future*. Maybe there was a chance for her happy ever after. She re-opened her eyes and gave her men a shy smile. Jack gently pushed his way into her body, stretching her. He pulled out a little before working his way back in, farther this time. He repeated this a few times before he'd completely filled her.

He stroked her cheek kissed her. "Be patient a little longer. We'll make it good, I promise."

He kept saying that, but they'd given her enough mind-blowing orgasms since they'd met, she had no trouble believing him. Hang on. Was that trust? Hell, who was she trying to kid? There was no way she'd be right here, right now, even with others in the house, if she didn't trust them.

"Jack, we'd best get this show on the road before our girl gets too bored and starts making a grocery list" Griff moved in behind Jack and winked. "Our girl might be getting slow and easy, but you aren't."

Griff's quick thrust pushed Jack's cock a little deeper and his groin pressed hard against Ella's clit. Griff pulled back as fast as he'd advanced, and the pressure against Ella's cervix and clit immediately eased.

Jack withdrew completely before starting another slow slide in. The moment he'd bottomed out, Griff slammed his hips home, and the pressure was back.

Fuck—it wasn't going to take too many more moves like this before they had her coming hard enough to see stars.

They only did it once more. This time, Jack didn't withdraw. Instead, he held still while Griff slammed into his ass, each thrust harder and faster than the last.

She could feel Jack's heart pounding against her chest as his breathing got faster. "Come when you're ready, love. Neither of us is going to be able to hold on much longer." He leaned in and claimed her mouth and it only took two more thrusts from Griff for her to come so hard she thought she might pass out. She had no idea how long she'd been making those ridiculous squealing pig noises before she clued in and snapped her mouth shut.

"How about that," Griff said as he flopped onto the bed, "our girl is a screamer."

Embarrassed, Ella looked away, but Jack caught her chin and turned her back to face him. "Don't hide from us, sweetheart." He grinned and gently pumped his hips a couple times. "You puffed our egos up by about three sizes. There's no shame in that. Okay?"

"Okay." She hoped she sounded more confident that she felt.

He kissed the tip of her nose, then reached between

them and slowly withdrew his still half-hard cock. "I have some cleaning up to do," he said as rolled to the side.

"No," Griff said, "you stay there with our girl, I'll take care of the clean up."

Jack removed the condom, tied it in a knot, and placed it in Griff's outstretched hand.

As Griff headed to the bathroom, Jack took Ella's hand in his and kissed it. "How are you doing, sweetness?"

"Wonderful." Holy hell, that was better than wonderful, it was amazing.

Then the doubt and insecurity started seeping in. She didn't remember them actually coming. Did they come? Was she so disgusting, they'd lost their erections? What if this was just some kind of twisted game? Maybe she should leave now. Dump them before they have the chance to dump her. Yeah, that was the best thing to do.

"Ella—stop" Jack wrapped her in his arms and held her close. "It's okay, sweetness. We're not going anywhere and you're safe."

"But you didn't come."

Jack gave a little chuckle. "Sweetie, there is no mistaking a well-used condom—and those were definitely well-used."

"Really?"

"We're going to have to work harder at convincing you that we're serious about you."

"We can start right now," Griff climbed on the bed and stroked the inside of her thigh. "Lift your leg, sweetheart."

After a ten year cock-hiatus, even that fairly gentle sex had left her a little sore and achy, and she appreciated Griff soothing her tender flesh with a warm, damp cloth.

Maybe that second orgasm should wait. She smiled and got the warm-fuzzies when she noticed he was cleaning Jack as well. So sweet.

When he was done, Griff flung the cloth across the room. "Score." He declared when it landed on the floor of the en-suite bathroom.

"You are such a child sometimes," Jack said.

"Sometimes," Griff agreed as he curled himself around Ella and Jack.

Ella snuggled in, absorbing the warmth and safety she felt being cocooned between these two sweet, sexy men.

As she drifted off to sleep, she considered how special they always made her feel and how gentle they were with her, and her final conscious thought was how much she wanted *this* every night.

# EPILOGUE



GRIFF PATTED his pocket for what must have been the hundredth time since he'd left home. The hand-crafted gold rings and necklace, all bearing the same triangular Celtic knot—a triquetra—hadn't disappeared since he'd last checked. *Was it really only five minutes ago?*

He thought back over the last few months. It had been one hell of an emotional roller-coaster, but the ups far outnumbered the downs.

Ella still had black moments of insecurity and self-doubt, but they worked through them as a family. He and Jack fully understood that the trauma Ella experienced followed by ten years of avoiding intimacy was not something she would fully move past quickly or easily—if ever.

And that was okay. They loved and accepted her for who she was.

He was relieved Sully had finally managed to pull his head out of his ass and sort things out with Ella, because it wouldn't have been right to do this without him.

His phone buzzed on the table. The text message was from Sully. *They're here.*

Show time.

———

ELLA TRIED to control her nerves as she and Jack waited for Griff to appear. Dammit, the way she was carrying on, you'd think she was getting married. Well, it wasn't *that* far off, when she thought about it. The only real difference was the legal stuff.

"Hey, it'll be fine. Nothing will change except we'll all have shiny new jewellery."

She looked up and smiled. Damn, he cleaned up well. "You two sneaky buggers wouldn't let me see—for all I know, it's something from a Christmas cracker."

"You know better." Jack put his arm around her shoulder and pulled her close. She wrapped her arms around his waist and squeezed him tight.

It was amazing what a few months with a couple of guys who really cared could do for a girl. It wasn't that long ago, she wondered what it would be like to be snarky like Mac. Well, not quite like Mac, that was living too close to the edge, but she liked the feeling of power it gave her.

They still kept their BDSM pretty light, and she

worried about that sometimes. She knew Griff and Jack had played hard before she came along, and while she still harboured the odd doubt that she was giving them what they needed, deep down, she did believe they accepted her as she was.

She looked over at Sully, thankful they'd managed to salvage their friendship. Ridiculous man—so in touch when it came to the needs of others, yet oblivious when it came to his own. She hoped he got his shit together and sorted things out with Teagan before it was too late.

A figure appeared in the doorway, and Ella looked over to see Griff walk in wearing a new suit and a big grin. Relief quieted her jangling nerves. Somewhere along the way, she'd had a small crisis of faith—terrified this was nothing more than an elaborate prank—and Griff's arrival made all that doubt vanish in an instant. Apparently, it was fear of rejection, not commitment that had twisted her up in knots.

Griff crossed the room and pulled Jack and Ella into a hug and asked, "Are we ready?"

They both nodded and they all turned to face their guests. Jack took Ella's left hand, Griff took her right, and in front of her, they held each other's. They were really going to do this.

---

JACK LOOKED at the two most important people in his life as he held their hands, and figured he had to be the luckiest bastard to roam the earth. The universe had come through on that seemingly impossible request and he was grateful. That morning, they'd drawn straws to decide who spoke first. Griff had drawn the short straw, and Jack was kind of glad Ella would speak last.

Griff cleared his voice and the room fell silent. "Jack, there was a time when I thought we weren't going to pull through. Those were dark, dark days for me. I was terrified of losing the one person I needed most in my life, but I was even more terrified to fight for him. What if he didn't want me? Then we met Ella, and in that moment, I knew I had to find my balls and fight for you." Griff cleared his throat as he bent his head and shrugged his shoulder to wipe away the tear running down his cheek. He gave Jack's hand a small squeeze and continued. "Ella, the first thing you ever gave me was hope. Since then, you've given me trust and love—precious gifts I hold close to my heart."

Jack took a deep breath and hoped he could keep his emotions in check until he'd said his piece. "Griff, my life with you has been incredible, and I didn't think it was possible to love you more. Then Ella came into our lives, and I discovered how wrong I was. Ella, you brighten my life in so many ways, but it's your trust and love that makes our family complete."

"Jack, Griff," Ella began, "your love and patience has been the lifeline I didn't realise I needed. I was drowning in a sea of loneliness until you came along and reminded me of what I was missing. More than that, you make me feel beautiful, safe, and loved. Three things I'd dismissed as unattainable." She looked first to Jack, then to Griff and said, "I'm yours."

Jack gave Ella a gentle kiss while he lifted her hair out

of the way for Griff to fasten the delicate chain around her neck. When Griff was done, he turned Ella to face him. He stroked her cheek, then brushed his lips over hers. Jack almost regretted having a formal commitment ceremony because he wanted nothing more than to drag Griff and Ella to bed and fuck them into oblivion. Instead, they still had to exchange rings and stay until it was socially acceptable to leave.

Ella took the first ring from Griff's outstretched hand. She rose up on her toes and kissed him as she placed it on his finger. Jack took the second and slipped it onto Ella's finger, then he gave her a deep, lingering kiss, a promise of all the good things to come. Jack was unprepared for the feeling of complete peace when Griff slid the remaining ring into place. They pulled Ella into a hug, then exchanged a passionate kiss of their own.

Jack held on tight to his family and wondered if it would be too greedy to ask the universe for more. Kids that looked like Griff and Ella, maybe. Someday.

## Tainted Pearl: A Rock Star Prequel

Lust at first sight has never been a problem for Doug Fraser before, but something about Biddy O'Mara screams "hands off". Except the private, mysterious musician is also the sexiest, most captivating woman he's ever crammed into close quarters with.

Biddy can't afford any distractions while on a month long eco-activism island adventure. The rock star is incognito for a very good cause, but the irresistible camera operator quickly proves a big, bad complication.

A fling is inevitable. But Doug's not relationship material, and the more he gets to know Biddy, the more he realizes she's the type of girl you take home to meet your mother—even if you don't know all her secrets.

# TAINTED PEARL: A ROCK STAR PREQUEL

## CHAPTER ONE

"Have you lost your fucking mind? We go on tour in barely six weeks and you decide to go play eco-terrorist? What if you get hurt? It's not like we can just order up a new bass player off the Internet, you know."

If there was one thing Biddy could count on, it was Honeycunt's compulsion to say exactly what she thought—Tainted Pearl's lead singer had absolutely no filter.

"Calm down, woman. I'm not an idiot. As much as I wanted to get in on the real action, fighting illegal fishing and whaling on an off-shore campaign wasn't a serious consideration. I'm going as an observer on a small island where they slaughter entire whale pods in the name of tradition. The sole purpose of the campaign is to document and share what we see with the world—it's strictly hands-off. The only action I'm going to see is what I capture through the lens of my camera."

"Jesus, Biddy, couldn't you just donate a fuck-load of money instead?"

"Of course I could, but that's way too easy. I want to feel like I'm doing something. Throwing money at an issue isn't enough for me, anymore."

Honeycunt reached over and patted Biddy's knee. "Sweetie, I know you mean well. Really, I do, but we're not just talking risk of injury, here. You could get arrested, and while that on its own could cause problems, if you got charged with a crime and convicted, that would totally fuck up your ability to travel for the rest of your life. You wouldn't be able to tour."

This was one thing Biddy hated about being in a band. Always having to weigh her personal wants against the best interests of the group. "Look, I've been through all this with Owen. He said all the concerned-manager things he gets paid for, and I promised all the good-client things necessary to keep his head from exploding. Honestly, I'll just be photographing events as they unfold. I won't be interfering in any way. It's a done deal and you're going to have to trust me. I leave tomorrow. If it makes you feel any better, I'll check in every day."

"You'd better. It won't stop me worrying, though."

"I know." Biddy glanced up at the clock. "Look, I need to get moving. I still have to pack."

"Do not take any chances." Honeycunt pointed her index finger at Biddy. "Not just because you'd fuck up the tour for the band, but because we love you and want you to be safe. Promise me."

"I'll be careful. I promise."
***

Biddy hadn't been surprised by the reaction of her band mate at all. Which was why she waited until the last possible minute to reveal her plans for the six week break between finishing their latest album and their next tour.

Normally when they were in between recording and touring, she'd spend her down-time doing risk-free activities like vegetating in front of the television and catching up on her reading.

She discovered the Red Earth Ninjas during their last break. She had fallen asleep in front of the TV and woken up in the middle of a documentary about the group of environmental activists.

By the time the show was over, she knew she wanted to help. She'd fired up her laptop and spent countless hours researching the group and their activities.

She'd already taken into account all the issues Honeycunt and Owen were concerned about. She'd thought long and hard about her decision, and she hadn't been bullshitting when she told them she would be staying out of trouble.

Risk of injury or a criminal record weren't the only things she'd be worried about. She'd struggled long and hard over whether to out herself to REN. Biddy valued her privacy above all else, and she worked very hard to keep her band persona, Boots, separate from who she was in real life. Boots was loud, flamboyant, and had a serious boot fetish—hence the nickname. Biddy was quiet, shy, and did her best not to stand out in a crowd.

In the end, she'd chosen to maintain her privacy. She was no different from any other volunteer who had a job to return to, and she didn't want to be singled out for special treatment. Besides, she didn't want REN to exploit her minor celebrity status. Yes, Boots could probably do a lot of good for the organisation by publicly endorsing it, but that wasn't what she was looking to achieve. Boots was taking a break and Biddy was going to use this time to be herself.

She checked her watch as she walked to her car. Running behind as usual. She mentally reorganised the tasks she still had to take care of before she flew out the next evening. Her ability to procrastinate was legendary, and no matter how hard she tried to get shit done well ahead of schedule, she always, always ended up banging hard up against deadlines. At least this time she wasn't scrambling to renew her passport before leaving the country.

Oh well, like the saying goes, if you leave it until the last minute, it only takes a minute. By her calculations, laundry was her number one priority—she wasn't going to risk being pulled aside by customs with a day-pack full of dirty underwear.

It was ridiculous that she had at least three loads of laundry to do before she could pack, but recording exhausted her and she was doing well if she managed to make it to her bed before falling asleep after each session.

At least she could handle most of her pre-trip business while her clothes were being washed and dried.

Fuck, if she were organised, she'd have just dropped it all off at a local laundromat and paid to have someone there do it while she was at the studio.

No. If she were organised, she'd have taken care of her laundry earlier. The last thing she needed was the laundry person figuring out who she was and selling her dirty panties online. Eew.

### One Gold Heart (Dominant Cord, Book 1)

Finn Taylor is an asshole. So why does he keep showing up in Mac's late-night fantasies as the Dom of her dreams? She can't even ignore him, because she's stuck working with the fellow musician for the Christmas concert season.

Mac Wallis is a mess, and Finn can't fall for a submissive who's so damaged she needs medication just to get through a performance. But he's drawn to the beautiful oboist, even as he keeps pissing her off. He can't resist trying to take care of her--in every way.

### One Gold Knot (Dominant Cord, Book 2)

*She didn't do relationships. She didn't even do all night.*

After years of avoiding her teenage crush, Hildy Klein is shocked to come face to face with Wilson Kennedy.

Her uncle's wake isn't the place to unravel all the ways that Wilson could leave her emotionally vulnerable and exposed, yet his gentle persistence is impossible to ignore.

But Wilson is no longer that boy in her fantasies, and now Hildy must decide if she will give up control and commit to the protective, kinky Dom he's become.

**Tainted Shadow (Tainted Pearl, Book 1)**

Tainted Pearl's lead singer has a stalker problem and bodyguard Brody Clarke doesn't think twice about cutting his vacation short when he's asked to protect her.

Sparks fly—and not the good kind—when he rubs the rabidly independent rock star the wrong way. Now he needs to convince her that letting him be in control might just save her life.

And if it has the side benefit of turning those sparks into a completely different kind of heat? Brody's up for that kind of dominance as well.


**Prime Minster (Frisky Beavers #1)**

Gavin:

Ellie Montague is smart, sensitive, and so gorgeous it hurts to look at her. She's also an intern in my office. The office of the Prime Minister of Canada.*

That's me. The PM.

She calls me that because when she calls me Sir, I get hard and she gets flustered, and as long as she's my intern, I can't twist my hands in her strawberry-blonde hair and show her what else I'd like her to do with that pretty pink mouth.**


Ellie:

How much I like the PM varies on a daily basis. He's intense, controlling, and a perfectionist in every way—and he demands the same of his staff.

How much I want him never wavers.

There's something about him that tugs at me deep inside, and makes me wish that just once he'd cross the line in a late night work session. I'd take that secret to the grave if it meant I got a taste of the barely restrained beast inside him.***

FOOTNOTES:

* This is a fictional erotic romance. No prime ministers or interns were harmed in the making of this book.

** Except it's a BDSM romance, so they were hurt a little.

*** Spoiler alert: she gets more than a taste. And she likes it.

## ACKNOWLEDGMENTS

Élianne Adams, Elizabeth Varlet, and Zoe York for their unwavering support and encouragement. Sidney Bristol for helping me find my way. Gia Alden for the last minute eagle-eye. The wonderful gang of Divas who are generous in so many ways. And of course, my wonderful, supportive husband, who still says yes to almost everything...except another dog.

## ABOUT THE AUTHOR

Surrounded by mist-covered mountains, Sadie Haller lives a quiet life with her husband and fur-babies.

*Where to find Sadie*

sadiehaller.com

sadie@sadiehaller.com

9 780099 382645 0